SURREALISTIC
MIDNIGHT RIDE

THOMAS MUHLRAD

iUniverse, Inc.
Bloomington

Surrealistic Midnight Ride

iUniverse books may be ordered through booksellers or by contacting:

iUniverse
1663 Liberty Drive
Bloomington, IN 47403
www.iuniverse.com
1-800-Authors (1-800-288-4677)

Because of the dynamic nature of the Internet, any web addresses or links contained in this book may have changed since publication and may no longer be valid. The views expressed in this work are solely those of the author and do not necessarily reflect the views of the publisher, and the publisher hereby disclaims any responsibility for them.

Any people depicted in stock imagery provided by Thinkstock are models, and such images are being used for illustrative purposes only.
Certain stock imagery © Thinkstock.

ISBN: 978-1-4759-3761-9 (sc)
ISBN: 978-1-4759-3768-8 (ebk)

Library of Congress Control Number: 2012912458

Printed in the United States of America

iUniverse rev. date: 10/15/2012

Thomas Muhlrad
500 West 235th Street Apt LG
Bronx, NY 10463
347 964 7257 You can leave a message.
Cell 646 355 9733 please don't hang up to soon; wait till I answer

Where the hell was I going to find a whore? Not in Scarsdale. There are no street whores in our little town of wealth and fame. I knew there were prostitutes in Manhattan but where in Manhattan? Hell with it I'll go to the City and take things from there. I picked up my cell phone and Palm Pilot. I couldn't do without the Palm Pilot; it held the passwords to my computer files at the office. I only had fifty dollars in cash. I had to get some real money.

I jumped into my Mercedes and drove to the bank's cash machine. I withdrew eight hundred bucks which maxed out my ability to get money from the ATM for the next twenty-four hours. No big problem, I had my credit cards and my checkbook. And if push came to shove, I could tap petty cash in the office.

I headed south for New York City. At 12:30 am in the morning the Saw Mill River Parkway is empty. I stepped on the gas pedal and moved at eighty-five miles an hour. I started enjoying myself. I was hunting for pussy for the first time in fourteen years. I didn't know where the woman I was looking for might be, but I'll find her.

A couple years ago I read in the New York Times that the 14th Street Meat Market area was ripe with prostitutes. They were serving late night truckers making beef deliveries to New York City. I decided to go there. In fifteen minutes I hit the Henry Hudson toll bridge. I paid the toll and cruised down the parkway totally empty except for a black Porsche. He was next to me in the right lane. I stepped on the gas pedal—the speedometer shot up to ninety miles an hour. He stayed nose to nose with me. At a hundred and ten miles an hour I chickened out. I slowed down to eighty-five miles an hour. The Porsche's driver flashed his brights and moved out at a hundred and twenty miles an hour; its red taillight faded in the distance in seconds. I have to get one of those cars but will I have the balls to drive it that fast? I didn't know but I felt great.

The traffic picked up around 57th Street no more joy rides here there were cops. I got off at the Meat Market exit but the streets were deserted just guys delivering meat. I decided to drive to 8th Ave and 42nd Street. It used to be a good place for peep shows and sex but that was before Disney came to town. What the hell I decided to give it try anyway. I cruised uptown. I arrived at 42nd street and 8th Ave in 10 minutes cruising at 35 miles an hour; I hit the traffic lights just right.

The lights were much brighter. The streets were full of people but I didn't see any whorish looking women. I reached across and rolled down the window on the passenger side. I got offers for marijuana, but no women. On my fourth time around the block a Police cruiser pulled behind me; the sudden whoop of its siren shook me up.

Two women cops got out of the car. One went to the passenger side, the other one came to the driver's side. Both had their hands on the butt of their guns. They asked for my driver's license and insurance certificate. The cop on my side went back to the cruiser while the other one was real tense staring me down. I looked away. I didn't want to get these policewomen nervous, rumors were that in New York City cops shoot first and frame you later. Finally, after ages it seemed to me, the other cop came back and handed me my papers. "So what brings you to Times Square at this hour, Mr. Goodwin?" My face flushed red, the first time since I had been a teenager. I stammered a lie. Both women cops relaxed and laughed too loud.

"I think he said he is looking for cheap sex, Sherry." The woman cop next to me said.

The crimson blush that just left my face returned in spades. I just sat there speechless.

"Look Joe I can call you Joe can't I? It's a good thing you didn't accept the offer of drugs, because you would have been on your way to night court and your little old Mercedes would have become city property." The cop next to me mocked.

Sherry asked. "I bet your wife threw you out?" Like an idiot I shook my head no and said yes, involuntarily. "Well Joe let me call you Joseph if you have the blues go to the West 72nd street area where there are plenty of New Age beer joints where you can drink your troubles away. You might even find a nice woman who will comfort you free of charge. You know what I mean Joseph?"

I bobbed my head up and down. The cop next to me started writing a ticket.

"This is for your left backup light, it's out. Just take the car up to the nearest NYC Police station after you have it fixed. It has to be done in the next 24 hours otherwise you will have to pay the fine."

I had to open my mouth. "I saw it just half an hour ago. It was . . ." I bit my tongue, because both cops tensed up.

"Which light is out Marcia?"

"The left rear light Sherry"

"Let me see it for myself."

"The left taillight . . . ." Sherry answered.

I felt a thump on the car and the sound of plastic hitting the pavement.

"Marcia the left rear light is definitely out."

Marcia handed me the ticket and in a motherly tone said, "Joseph all kidding aside, you have to be out of your mind, to have sex with street whores. They all have AIDS they really do Joseph. Your wife may give you a second chance, AIDS does not."

And with that they were gone. Fuck them. Some joke. I got out of the car and looked at the totaled taillight. It will cost me five-hundred bucks to replace it. For a second I was thinking of going home but the humiliation of the last thirty odd days ate at my guts. I am going to find company. I aimed the car for the West Side highway and up to Seventy-second St, what better recommendation, then those fricking cops. With the way my luck was running I'll find a tavern with beer guzzling women cops, who handcuff you, before sex. A little voice in the back of my mind kept saying. "Things look less and less promising." I decided if this 72nd Street trip doesn't workout I would head for home like a whipped dog. Wet old dog at that, it started drizzling.

I lucked out. There was a parking spot just as I got off at the 72nd Street exit from the West Side Highway. There was an adrenal surge as I pulled into it; I was ready to challenge any one making a move, for the parking place. I set there super satisfied, I got the space. In my satisfaction I realized what a Pavlovian' animal I was, it was early in the morning with no other cars in sight, yet I was in total battle mode for the parking spot no one was contesting, I began to think I needed to have my head examined.

I walked down to Broadway and 72nd street and I didn't see anything resembling a club. A bum walked up to me and said. "No whores in this part town man."

I got pissed.

"What the hell makes you think I am looking for a whore?"

"I live on the street man. I see millions of people. You are looking for loving."

"Ok! Here's twenty bucks if you show me where I can find a hot Club."

He grabbed for the twenty, but I held onto it.

"Ok! Ok! You see that furniture store and the Deli next to it?"

I said. "Yeah."

"Well in between them is a stairway that leads up to 'One Plus One Equals Three' Club. Some hot putang go in and out of there. It's an all night joint but you got to work for the pussy man, it's a legal club. No whores, not the type who want money, anyway."

I let go of the twenty and asked him, "Putang? Were you in the service man?" He answered; "Yeah."

"What branch?"

"The Salvation Army branch." He cracked up with laughter and shuffled away.

"Ok! One point for the bum and zero points for the shmuck. He at least had a sense of humor."

I skipped up the stairs. I expected a bouncer or something but the door opened to a big barroom. The stale smell of beer smelled great. There were people around the bar and the hubbub of voices sounded friendly. There seemed to be as many women as men, a good sign from my point of view. I found a spot by the bar and ordered a Michelob for eight dollars a bottle, I thought it was pretty expensive, but I was here to enjoy myself and that was the price. I took a deep sip of the beer and let out a deep sigh and took in the place. It was a big room. There was a smallish dance floor. A couple of guys were dancing with each other, but most of the dancers were men and women. It was lively and everyone seemed to be happy, just a place to kick back and relax.

I spotted an empty table. I picked up my beer and headed for the table. Before I could get comfortable a woman said. "If you stay you will have to pay rent, this is my table."

I looked up expecting an argument but when I saw her the only thing I could say stupidly under my breath was. "I want to rent it as long as you sit with me."

She was stunning. Straight Platinum Blond hair cut down to her shoulders. She wore an almost see-through white silk blouse, nipples jutting through. Her tan leather pants fit just right, not cheaply tight, yet it followed her curves comfortably; she could have stepped out Vogue. But it was her heart shaped face I fell in love with right then and there. Big, translucent brown eyes, with a hint of eye shadow on the lids. She wore no other makeup except for fiery rich red lipstick on her lips. I inhaled her essence, it was spring Lilac. She frowned.

"We will discus how long a lease you get later. Now first let's talk rent. A double Manhattan will be a good start and for you a double Martini."

so hard. She and Jack West were tied together until somebody separated them, because I had the handcuff key. I felt a lot better; a hell of a lot better. I also found her cell phone.

I dialed my buddy Nathan who worked for the Scarsdale Tattler. He lived a couple of houses down the block from me. The commotion caused by the sirens and his natural nosiness should have gotten him over to my house, I wanted to hear his report. Everybody loved Nathan on the street but we all knew for a story he would rat on his mother, or so he said.

"Hello! Nathan?"

"Yeah! Who is this?" After a second, "is that you Joe?"

I hate being called Joe but Nathan doesn't give a shit he keeps calling me Joe. I tried to figure out a way to play with his name but Nathan is Nathan. Joe sounded pretty good compared to Nathan.

I said. "Yes."

"Where the hell are you?" He asked.

"I am on the way to Manhattan. I got some business I have to finish." I replied.

"Man you came close to being framed for attempted murder." Nathan said in a sanguine voice.

Then he started his spiel.

"Here is how it went. I was walking the dogs when I heard a shot and saw the lights in your house go out. I called the cops on my cell phone. I though you were being robbed.

"It's kind of early to walk your dogs isn't it Nathan?" I asked.

"No it's not, that is time when I walk them. Then he said.

"You want to shut up and let me tell you what happened after you left your house; pretty fast if I recall. I thought you shot your wife."

I said.

"We know each other since pre K and you haven't changed. You are the first one in line to screw me. What would make you think I would shoot my wife?"

"You want to hear the story or not Joe?" he said. "Besides who ratted me out to Mrs. Krieg in kindergarten, because I spilled my milk in the flower pot. She made me drink another container of milk; I still hate milk."

With mounting anger I said.

"I was five years old and so were you and the plant stunk for weeks; for God's sake man what in hell made you think I would shoot Ursula?"

"If you let me go on with the story Joe, things will become clear."

"Sure go on," I said.

"I went back to my house and put on my special baseball cap with the camcorder in it." Nathan bragged.

"But before we go on with the story Joe, I am sorry to say Jack West has been screwing your wife for the last two months or so. You go to work and they get together for a couple hours. Everybody in the neighborhood knows but you Joe."

"Why didn't you tell me Nathan?" I asked. His words were like a wound in my side.

"That is easier said than done compadre. Lots of friendships are lost telling friends about things they may not want to hear. And to tell you the truth I didn't give a shit. So, she was getting a little on the side, admittedly doing it with Jack was obnoxious, but today's liberated woman does whatever she wants."

"Bullshit Nathan. You didn't tell me, because you are afraid of Jack."

"No, I am not." He said little too fast. "It is my mortgage that I am afraid of, losing my job is what I am scared of. I got two teenage kids in private schools and they both want to go to Yale. I need my job period. I am the managing editor of the paper but I don't own it."

"What the hell does West have on you Nathan?" I asked.

"Nothing it's my fricking Boss. He and Jack are the best of friends. You ever meet Phil Weld the CEO and fifty one percent owner of the Tattler?"

"Yes, I talk to him every time you throw a big party. A, boisterous prick, when he has a few." I said.

"Well his sixteen year old son hit and killed a pedestrian on the Post Road intersection, Baby Weld the apple of his father's eye was dead drunk and he only had a learner's permit.

Jack West was first on the scene. To make a long story short Jack faked the breathalyzer and the kid walked. It took a little doing because Fat Ass Mary also answered the call. She is honest but after twenty years on the Scarsdale Police force she sees nothing, hears nothing and fucks nothing. All she cares about are her mongrel Chihuahuas. She keeps showing them but ten years and not a ribbon. It didn't take Jack very much effort to convince Mary that the Kid was in shock not drunk.

Mary clicked into her see nothing, say nothing, and hear nothing, mode and followed the ambulance with the corpse to the hospital; allowing Jack to handle the kid. Jack drove the boy home. Phil Weld was *would cause further foolhardy investments; like in Indonesia. The essence of your article is that the scheme is wide open to corruption. You are right Nathan. It is corruption but that's the bloody point Nathan, the whole point."*

"People make tons of money when there is corruption. Clinton must have understood that on the spot, a very bright man. When we from Harvard presented the international economic plan to him, Clinton loved the inclusion aspect of helping third world people with new jobs. He understood the corruption aspects, because he introduced us to a bunch of contributors who wanted us to explain to them how scheme worked. The first question these Clintonite's asked us how much money did the World Bank cover in private foreign loses. We told him as much as the President puts in the kitty. They loved it and still love it."

Howard finished his salad and said.

"Here is the point that concerns you Nathan. We knew there would be a lot of criticism from the press. The thing is too transparent even for the economically blind American press. We put Clinton on it. We told the President the scheme would have to be scrapped if there was a lot of media pressure. We gave Clinton a diagram of the key players in Hollywood. He charmed and threatened and bribed the gay media machine to stay in line."

"We sent a bill to congress that made the media companies a mint, the media moguls couldn't jump on the bandwagon fast enough. If a Hollywood type did not hold the line Clinton's gay women battalions like that broken down old hag Barbara Strand ostracized that person until he or she got the message."

"It gets rough. You saw what happened to your Boss. He was kicked out so fast he thought he had a second asshole. Getting kicked out of the White House's social scene gets around fast. Women won't invite you to their socials, believe me it's a major disaster for the ostracized person's family and business. Falling from the A list to the shit list is major trauma. Clinton delivered the media for us and we are all getting very rich. The economic scheme goes on and will continue to go on Nathan; either you will hop on the bandwagon or you stay fired. Nobody wants to be brought down by negativism."

"What the hell do you get out of this?" I asked Howard with awe.

"For one I go to the White House when I want. Not in the Lincoln bedroom mind you but the economic council meetings. The President presides. He is interesting. At first I thought he was listening to every word and understood but I caught on to his act after the second meeting, he plays back what you say with a slight variation. My student essays are full of that type of chicanery. After one of the council meetings the President and I shook hands; he held on

18

to my hand little too long. I thought it was a joke, because he squeezed my hand real hard."

"What did you do?"

"I should have known better but I thought it was kind of sexual so I gave his hand a bone crunching squeeze; he winced. I am a couple of inches taller and hell of lot stronger, I play polo now. The horses bang you about but it's healthy. He let go but after that it was not Howey the economic maestro who could make tons of bloody money for his pals but a cool Howard."

"He stopped inviting my wife and me to White House dinner parties. That hurt because Millie likes the high life. He even stopped inviting me to the White House business luncheons."

"He changed his mind when he got a call from Treasury informing him that the English representative on the World Bank Board would vote negative for bailing out a Chinese group of investors from Indonesia. The Chinese investors were very close to President Clinton. Treasury dropped my name half a dozen times saying I was dear to the English Representative on the World Bank. The President's assistant got the message. I was back on the White House A list and I am staying there."

"You know how much I made last year Nathan? Three hundred million dollars; I paid less than two percent tax using offshore companies; the year before I made a hundred million. I don't know what to do with all that money. Getting back on the White House A list cost me 10 million pounds. I donated the money to the Queen's favorite Charity; herself. One of her economic advisors wanted to know why the sudden generosity."

"I told him the reason and the solution to the problem. Next day the U.S. Treasury Secretary called the White House and I was back on the A list, because the Indonesian Chinese Investment Group was in dire straits again; the bloody blokes kept losing money faster than their government could borrow from the World Bank to bail them out."

"Clinton keeps his distance from me but he is a realist. He accepts what he can't change. By the way I am not an official part of the government. The government doesn't pay me. I can make money any way I want."

"Have you got 10 million pounds Nathan to correct a mistake like I made. Finally Nathan are you getting the picture, is it simple enough for you? We don't want clever newsmen rocking the boat, because we have been friends for a long time I will get your job back Nathan but as a police reporter. It will be the same money you earn now."

"Fuck you Howard that's a young reporter's job not a guy my age."

"I will guarantee he won't fire you for five years."

"What is the point of this Howard? You want send me to purgatory?"

"No, but I ran a socio-economic model of Scarsdale, because of its wealth looking for buttons to push. To our surprise we found that some of the cops were very rich. I shut down the project, because we did not want to disturb the sub-culture, some of the richest families in the world live there. We did not want to poke a hornet's nest. You get my drift Nathan. Working with the cops you will get in the soft underbelly of Scarsdale; that is how the cops are getting rich."

"I see your scheme Howard. Maybe it could work. Are you sure about the millionaire cops?"

"Yes, the most notorious is a guy named Jack West, money in ten different banks with the same Social Security number but different names. He pays taxes. He must be sure of himself. Find out how he does it and you may get your own seed money Nathan then come and play with me for high stakes."

Howard swallowed an oyster.

"What? He lives on my block." I said truly surprised.

After a pause for the fresh bite of rich Harvard food I said.

"OK Howard; I will take the deal. Shit it's a challenge. If a prick like Jack West could make millions then I could too."

"That day, meeting Howard I became greedy Joe. I didn't go to the police station but I did start questioning the kid who was assigned to the desk. I didn't get anything until I met Fat Ass Mary at a dog show. She has the three monkey's attitude far as her colleagues went but as I said she will let out snippets of information for good press coverage of her dogs."

"Shit it's some story. How come I didn't know that you were fired?" I asked Nathan.

"I didn't tell anyone, because I did not want my wife Maggie to know, anyway thanks to the tape I made today you are free and clear Joe. Ursula won't get a dime from you. No alimony, not the house, nothing." Nathan told me in an exhausted voice.

"What happened to Howard?"

"He went back to England; filthy rich. He is Sir Howard now."

"How did Jack West make his millions?"

"I don't know for sure but I think he sells information and does favors for economic gangsters. He has contacts on all levels of government; city, state, federal and the military. Wherever there is law enforcement our Jack West has a friend. Now he will include me and tell me everything."

"He deserves you. I'll cut a check for ten thousand and send it to you at the Tattler Nathan. Meanwhile I am going to stay at my brother's house in the city. Thanks Nathan. I will keep in touch. Knowing how Jack West became a millionaire is worth the ten thousand. I love ya."

Nathan became alarmed.

"You are not going to do something stupid and blow the setup for me, will you Joe? Just when I got the proof I need to squeeze Jack. Do me a favor Joe don't interfere."

"Stop groveling Nathan. You just squeeze him good. Leave him high and dry, the fucker robbed my wife."

I didn't wait for his answer. I rolled down the widow and tossed out the phone and my marriage with it. Unexpectedly, deep sobs came from deep in my chest. I pulled the car over to the side and cried my heart out.

It took a little while to calm down. I wiped my eyes and drove off the shoulder into traffic. I reached the 72nd street exit in a half hour. I was hoping that the club was open. I found a parking place and walked to the One plus One makes Three club. I went inside. The room was crowded with people having their ham and eggs with their first glass of beer. I asked Carmine the bartender for my cell phone and Palm Pilot. He pointed to the last booth. Out the corner of my eye I looked to see if Brown was there, to my relief Brown was not in the bar. I walked to the booth that was set off to the side. Crystal was in there with a big pile of money and a calculator, she was counting. I sat down and looked at her with out saying a word. She pushed the Palm Pilot and cell phone toward me.

"I knew you would come back, Joseph." She said.

"Why are you counting money Crystal?"

"I told you I own these tables. Carmine owns the bar and I own the tables. We split the cost of the rent etc . . ."

I was glad to see Crystal. The night's pressure drained away from me. I slumped in the booth and watched her count the money. There must have been eight thousand dollars. She made two piles of bills. She asked me for my cell phone. She called Carmine who was at the bar. He came over did a quick count of the money and initialed an invoice and then left with a pile of cash.

The other pile of money went into Crystal's Lord and Taylor shopping bag. She rummaged in her purse and came up with an aluminum foil envelope. She rolled up a hundred dollar bill and told me to take a sniff.

"He was a very clever man. He knew every con game there was but lately he has been getting mean and now here he is, worm food." Crystal said without emotion.

"He was an asshole." Suki said. She was back totally naked. "He thought he could out smart everybody. He couldn't outsmart Death."

She spit toward Brown's body, the spit missed but her point did not.

"If he went to hell he is probably trying hustle the devil." Crystal said.

"He hustled nobody. He just had a big mouth. Let me tell you the cause of his demise." Suki said angrily.

"Do you know Pool Hall Johnny, Crystal?"

"I know he was Brown's partner. All I know he was a white guy who was a fantastic pool player, made a lot of money for Brown, who backed him. And since I loaned the money to Brown I made a lot of money also. I tried to meet him a couple of times but Brown always had an excuse why I shouldn't. Last year I put a lot of pressure on Brown for an introduction. He broke down and told me he would never introduce us, because he was afraid of being cut out of the deal. It made sense I stopped bugging him about Johnny."

"What you don't know." Suki said. "That he is a big deal among the pool hall crowd in Chinatown. The Chinese gangster boys accept Pool Hall Johnny as a regular guy. The money boy's took Johnny's word that Brown's word was good and that Brown had a lot of money."

"On the strength of Johnny's word, Brown was allowed to gamble with the Chinese big money boys. It's not easy to break into Chinese society so Pool Hall watched his Ps and Qs and played it straight with the Chinese money guys. Johnny was accepted by the Chinese, because his Chinese wife is well connected in Chinese society."

"Pool Hall was the only American man she ever met. One day she waited on him in her father's restaurant. She fell madly in love with him right then and there. She had sex with him then had her mother hassle Johnny until he married her. Johnny hung around Good Luck Pool Hall while she supported their two kids working for her father. She never complained, because she was proud of him. Johnny had a good reputation among the Chinese as a reliably guy. She had one mantra."

"Don't do anything stupid, nothing that will lose my father's family prestige."

"He saw the wisdom of her words and was honest in his dealings with the Chinese. His word is good as gold among the tough Chinese gangsters."

"Johnny met Brown when Brown was hustling suckers with Three Card Monty played on cardboard boxes, many years ago. Johnny watched Brown blow up from a two-bit hustler to a well-dressed high roller. Brown could drop hundred thousand on a boxing match and not think twice about it. So when Brown offered to bankroll Johnny with big bucks; Johnny accepted without much thought."

"The two of them went to New Jersey where Johnny was not that well known. Johnny never suckered players by losing a game or two. He made it no secret that he was a good player looking for action. His opponents walked away with lighter wallets but with the feeling that another day they could beat Johnny."

"He and Brown pulled in six to seven thousand a night. Brown told Johnny it was chicken feed compared to what they could make in the Good Luck Pool Hall. For weeks Brown was bragging that Pool Hall Johnny could beat anyone in the Good Luck Pool Hall. He bragged everywhere he gambled in Chinatown and how he had a million dollars to prove it. He dared any one to put up the money and play Johnny. As I said Johnny always made people feel that they could win the next game. The Chinese Gangster's considered and accepted the bet. But, they wanted to see the million. It had to be brought to the pool hall."

"Brown had a friend who replenished ATM machines. Brown paid him 10,000 dollars to show the gangsters a million dollars in twenties. It was very impressive. Brown and the hulking black man who carried a suitcase with one hand and a submachine gun in the other walked into Good Luck Pool Hall. The big guy didn't say a word. He opened the suitcase for everyone to see and counted out a million in twenties."

He looked at Brown and asked, "are they satisfied Brown?"

"No." One of the boy's said "lets see if they are real or not." Brown told the gangster.

"Take a thousand from any pile and check with the bank."

The boy said.

"That won't be necessary I will check the watermarks if they are there we can do business."

"Is that what the big Boss' says?"

"The Boss is the big man in Chinatown in the legal and the illegal world." Suki continued excitedly.

Coming out of the shadow the boss said.

"Yes, if the watermarks are there it's on."

cushions and knocking the two ball in the far corner pocket. The cue ball stopped in perfect position back of the four ball, an easy shot to the side pocket. Cue ball stopped in perfect position for a corner shot at the five ball. Her positioning of the cue ball was so good that every shot went in with ease. She did not use bank shots unless she had to, she went for the easy shots the winning shots, she was a marvel to watch. Between racks she just stood there drinking Avion water as if nothing special was happening. Johnny's face was ashen.

"By the third rack I moved away from Johnny and Brown. By the fourth rack I was standing next to the Boss." Suki said happily telling the story.

The Boss asked me what nationality was I. I told him. "Japanese and I bet you would like to tie me up—ha."

He laughed and said. "Yes; but tell me about your friend Brown."

"He is strictly thrills. He has no mother, no father, no girl friend, no boy friend just the desire to make money. He told me he hasn't had sex in ten years, a waste of time he said. Being with Brown is thrills, like tonight. But I think Brown bit off a bit more then he can chew." I told the Boss.

"Yes." the Boss said. "But lets watch the game."

Annie won. Rack after rack precision placing won it for her; if people came to see fancy shooting they were disappointed, she positioned the cue ball to make the shots to the pockets mundane. She won without Johnny getting a chance to shoot.

Pool Hall Johnny collapsed into his suit. Someone sent for his wife, crying she came and took him home. But before he left he told Brown.

"Your million had better be there or we are both in a lot of shit."

The Boss called Annie over and gave her a check for ten thousand dollars. Annie accepted it matter-of-factly. But when he gave her a silver trophy inscribed, Annie Chow the Best Pool Shark in New York and the World. She jumped up and down with tears of happiness running down her cheeks. She was one happy kid.

"The Boss had the pool hall cleared of everybody except his entourage and Brown. I was in the Boss's entourage. I learned where the power was real fast. I'll chow down on that old man any time." Suki laughed.

He walked over to Brown slowly when he reached him he said in a whisper that you could hear all over the pool hall.

"You owe me a million dollars Mr. Brown."

"No I don't, because I never saw that girl in the pool hall before."

"Yes you did. I have some photos here, is that you and her together?"

"Yes she looks like she is asking me for something. I have no recollection of it." Brown said with bravado.

"She was asking for chalk Mr. Brown." The Boss said.

"How many times did these encounters happen?" Brown asked, his voice unsteady.

"We have a dozen photographs and a surveillance camera tape of you two making contact." The Boss said without humor. "You are like a pointer dog Mr. Brown nothing can distract you from the hunt. I am like a fox, I would have wondered why this girl keeps popping in my face if for nothing else but for my vanity."

"We figured you would not notice her, she had nothing you wanted. We were counting on that Mr. Brown. She is a regular player on girl's tables in fact she has been a regular here since she was six. We covered every angle Mr. Brown, I want my money."

Brown started blustering but there was nothing to say.

"Ok," Brown said. "Take the damn suitcase." He headed for the door. When he reached the door a guy confronted him with a machine gun. "What do I do with him Boss?" The Chinese guy asked. There was a quick exchange words between the Boss and his associates in Chinese. One of the associates answered.

"Hold him there until we count the money. Be careful he is a professional boxer. If he tries anything funny shoot him in the legs the Boss wants him alive."

"Ok," He said. He stepped back a few steps and squatted on his heels. He aimed his machine gun straight at Brown's chest.

The guy with the gun said. "We might as well relax boy, it takes a long time to count a million bucks."

"Last time a guy called me 'boy' I kicked his teeth down his throat. You know what I mean Chink?" Brown hissed with a low threatening voice.

The Chinese guy didn't say anything back but he reached into his backpack and pulled out a machine gun silencer. He stepped back a few more steps and said.

"We will see who says what Brave Heart."

He leveled the gun on Brown's crotch.

"That is where the first shot is going if you make a move chum."

"You may hit me in the dick but that is the last shot you fire before I knock your head off." Brown said softly.

"Poof" Spat the machine gun. The bullet landed inches from Brown's ear in the wall.

One of the Boss's man ran over and said.

"Hey! The Boss says don't harm him yet if he runs then shoot him in the leg. You understand Nguyen?"

"Ok, Ok, I'll do it the Boss's way." He said pointing the gun at Brown's legs. To Brown the boss's man said.

"All these Vietnamese Chinese want to do is kill. So Brown you stay put. He may miss you leg and shoot you in the head. Counting is over real soon."

After a while the Boss's man said in a loud voice.

"Nguyen bring him here."

"I ain't moving until you get this son of a bitch off me." Brown said in a hushed voice.

"Stand six feet behind him Nguyen. That's OK Brown?"

"No! I want him away from me period." Brown said.

"You cut the bullshit Brown and come here. If you think you can run away forget it. I got three men like Nguyen outside." the Boss's men said. Two million dollars in the pool hall is a lot of money. Every thief in the world knows about it so we protect it."

Brown shrugged and walked over to the pool table where they were counting the money.

"Well Mr. Brown the final tally is two hundred thousand U.S. dollars and eight hundred thousand Kinko copy machine dollars." the Boss said with a vicious twist in his voice.

Brown was about to say something but the Boss said.

"I don't want to hear a word from you. None of your lies, none of your con bullshit, you will listen to me. You got twenty four hours to come up with the money otherwise you are dead as roast duck on a hook."

"OK, Boss I'll get the money in twenty four hours." Brown said visibly shaking.

The Boss without a word turned around and left through the back door.

"The Boss told me to come to him when his man was finished with Brown. I thought it was a little bit of an insult, because I like to walk out on the arm of a champion. On the other hand the air was electric in the pool hall I didn't really mind staying." Suki said.

The Boss's number one man Young made a call on his cell phone and then told Brown.

"I just called Pool Hall Johnny. He will work with you and Chin."

"Who the hell is Chin?" Brown blustered.

"That's Chin." Pointing to a giant Chinese' man who was 6'7" and all muscle, he was wearing motorcycle boots and worn dungarees. His black tee shirt was lettered.

"Electronic wizard," And under it in tiny letters it said. "There isn't a lock I can't fix."

"You a safe cracker Chin?" asked Brown

"You got to know how to get in them, to fix them." Chin said with a grin.

Out of the shadows cast by the pool table lights, looking like a ghost, Pool Hall Johnny entered. He walked up to Brown and said.

"We have been partners for a long time Brown but I got family here in China town, it's them or you. So partner you better believe I will kill you if you don't have the money in twenty four hours. Otherwise I am to help you in every way to get the money."

"We will get the money," Brown said, "I know this rich lady who has a nice safe."

"That broad you are always bragging about? The one who lives on the West Side?" Johnny asked. His voice was shaking like a leaf.

"Yeah! It's a shame, because she has been good to me. She was the person who opened the world of the high rollers for me. She put up the seed money for the car, clothing, apartment and living money for a year for a mere twenty percent of the take."

"That's all I know about Mr. Big Mouth Brown's bragging." Suki said. "Because at that moment the Boss asked for me, an old Chinese woman took me to his room. The woman whispered.

"The Boss don't like bad language."

"I'll remember to use some," I said laughing.

"The woman giggled like jackass. The room was sparse, a bed, a table, couple of wooden chairs, and a bunch of rope at the foot of the bed. He had me sit on one of the chairs and tried to tie me to it. He failed and said.

"I can't seem to do it maybe you can teach me by doing it on me?"

I looked in his eyes and knew what he wanted. I hog-tied him so tight he couldn't breath. I climbed on the bed and made him eat me while I was calling him every dirty name I could think off. When his little wang got hard I whacked him with my hands until he came. He was one happy

Boss. I untied the rope real slow. He got hard again. I gave him a rough hand job, he came a ton. When he was dressed I reached into my purse and gave him two hundred dollars and said.

"Best sex I had in a long time, Boss."

The Boss laughed so hard he had tears coming out of his eyes.

"You want to go hang out with me Suki?" The Boss asked.

I said. "Sure Boss."

We went to a bar where everybody knew him.

"This guy is influential. He owns a bit of every store in China Town; some kind of insurance deal. They pay insurance and he smiles on them kindly. He has to look invincible though, that explains elaborate con he pulled on Brown."

"The Boss told me he lost fifty thousand dollars to Brown in twenty five minutes playing poker. If Brown would have kept his mouth shut, and let it be, nothing would have happened to Brown. But Brown bragged all over the pool hall how he suckered the Boss. The Boss knew Brown was baiting him to get into another game which he didn't want to do, but he could not ignore the affront to his name. Boss had the Chinese Society's bail bond's man check Brown's police record. The guy found that Brown was arrested once for hustling a bunch of sailors for a thousand dollars at Three Card Monty. Brown was a card cheat. The Boss decided to get even."

I told the Boss.

"Brown is just plain stupid. He never knows when to quit."

"That's too bad," The Boss said, "Because it's the last time he cheats me."

"I am going to spank you Boss if you don't stop talking about Brown. Talk about me I am sexier." Suki said.

Boss's eyes started shinning and he said. "Lets go back to the apartment."

"When we got there I pulled my skirt way up to my waist so he could get a good look at my bush. He dropped his pants and underwear. He leaned over the bed and I gave him a beating with a slipper that left his ass purple. He turned around with a heavy hard on. I gave him another rough hand job. He sighed when he came. I pulled myself together and handed him one of my gold rings. He wanted to know why, I said.

"I am generous with men who give me a good time. Boss you gave me a good time."

"It seems kind of upside down to me. Are you going to come to see me again Suki?" The Boss asked almost shyly.

"I will Boss. You are my kind of man." I kissed him on the nose and I was out the door.

"I walked over to the Good Luck Pool Hall but it was empty. I went to an all night Chinese restaurant. A nice looking Chinese guy tried to hit on me but I was waiting for something and he was not it. Brown called on the cell. He said he scored big. He had enough to pay off the Boss and plenty more and would I like a paid trip to Las Vegas."

"If you do? Meet me at Kennedy Airport at 11.00 am." Brown said in his bragging voice.

I said. "Sure thing Brown Sugar, anything you want. China town is played out anyway."

"Tell me about it." Brown said.

That's the last I heard from Mr. Big Mouth Brown.

"What time did he call you and why didn't you warn me he lost a million dollars?" Crystal asked.

"He called me around six thirty. I warned you a couple of years ago he was a sleaze bag Crystal. You told me to butt out and mind my own business. I did." Suki hissed.

"How come you are so popular with the Chinese?" Crystal asked ignoring the hissing.

"I speak fluent Mandarin and Cantonese with a Japanese accent which makes them laugh and I am a good time girl, happy combination, brings lots of good luck."

Crystal turned toward me and asked.

"What time did you leave here Joseph? I mean after you had the fight with Brown."

"I don't know Crystal, three. It couldn't have been later than four thirty." I said. "What happened after I left?"

"Brown was real nice. He cleaned up. That was a nasty cut you gave him Joseph. He offered to give the money back. I didn't take it back, deal is a deal. He wanted to know what I was going to do the rest of the night. I told him I would be at the club till ten in the morning so I could count the receipts. He told me he had some business downtown but would see me in the afternoon and left. That was around four a.m."

"Looking back with hind sight he didn't come here to play the con game at all. He was checking to see if the apartment was empty. But that was Brown he could jump into an act in a second." Crystal said.

on the extra electronics I put in those machines. I started following Jamal on his route when one of my ATM's alarm went off. I opened couple of machines after Jamal left and counted the money; it was short. He was short changing five hundred ATM machines."

"I called the Boss's number one man Young Wong and asked him what to do. He told me to follow Jamal to his apartment take the money back and fire him. I thought that was too risky. I thought I should build a police case against him and let the Insurance Company pick up the tab. Young told me to keep it quiet and not to mention it to the Boss. That Young Wong is a real rat. He has fifty ways of covering ass."

"I followed Jamal to Broadway and Houston where he picked up Mr. Brown then they drove to the Good Luck Pool Hall. Brown showed us our money and everybody was cheerful and happy. After Brown left I told the Boss that the money they showed was ours; the Associations. The Boss went pale. Without a word he left, Brown suckered him again."

"Young Wong took over and hired those crazy Vietnamese Chinese to prevent Mr. Brown from walking away after the game. Jamal put the money as he and Brown planned back in the machines. But the getting the money back didn't help the Boss; he lost a lot of face. He hired me to make sure you and Brown understood that you two had to come up with the money. Meanwhile the old men, the top tier of the Association, were thinking out loud that they may have to look around for another Boss to run things. You want to guess who might become the next Boss?"

"I don't keep up with Association politics, who?" Pool Hall answered in a whining voice.

"Your son's great grandfather."

"Oh him; Granddad Lu, He refuses to speak to my wife for marrying me but he has the kids over every weekend. I didn't know he was such a high person in the Association." Pool Hall Johnny said relaxing visibly.

"My advice to you Johnny is to take the two million to the pool hall and let the Boss come and get it from you. Stay there for twenty-four hours if Young Wong does not show up to collect it in twenty-four hours go home and give it to your wife. It means Mr. Lu won the battle against the Boss. The battle started when we left Chinatown. Mr. Lu thought you deserved to be beaten by that girl but it was unfair to hold you responsible for Brown's shenanigans. The Boss should have warned you that Brown didn't have the million. You could have called off the game saving face for everybody, after all you are member of an influential Chinese family."

"I am going to inform the Boss and Mr. Lu that you were in on the killing and that you put two bullets in Brown's chest. That should give you some sort of prestige with them. Right now your reputation is low as the side walk"

"What about the girl where the hell did she learn to play pool like that?" Johnny asked.

"From you Johnny; Annie had a crush on you when she was eight years old. The only way she thought she could get close to you is to play good pool. It turns out she has this incredible talent for pool. The Boss wants to send her to Las Vegas for the Women's World Pool Championship. Her Parents won't hear of it, they want her to stay in High School to become a doctor."

Pool Hall was going to ask some more questions but Chin interrupted him.

"I keep looking at that safe and there is something funny about it. It has very little depth for its size. I bet there is something the back of it."

"I bet it's a pin hole lock again but where? Johnny hand me the flashlight. Chin used the flashlight to search the safe door first he didn't find anything. Mumbling to himself he said.

"Maybe I am on a wild goose chase."

Running his finger on the bottom shelve of the safe he felt an indentation and a hole. He stuck the ice pick in the hole and a handle popped out from the side of the safe. Chin pulled on it and the first safe moved up to the ceiling revealing a safe that looked ultra modern shinny and impregnable.

"Thank God it's a Schnorf safe." Chin said. "I worked on this type of safe when I went to locksmith school in Germany. Johnny Get me my tool kit. I will have the safe open in fifteen minutes. By the way Johnny if that broad walks in here shoot her no hesitation."

"Don't worry." Johnny said. "Brown said Crystal never comes home before ten a.m."

"It's 7:13 am. I will have this baby open by 7:55 the latest meanwhile look around for big garbage bags to carry the stuff we find in this safe. It is a big one."

The tape stopped. I looked at Suki who was fascinated by what was happening on the screen. I looked at Crystal she was totally insane. Her eyes were blood shot. She bit her lips so hard that blood was trickling down her chin. She was ripping ribbons in the bed cover with her clinched fist. Despite that she looked marvelous, considering there was a dead man under the bed.

She hissed.

"That bastard ripped off my mother's jewelry collection. Mommy was crazy about jewelry. In twenty five years she put together a collection rivaling the richest princes of Europe and on top of that the bastard ordered my death as if I was just a fish in a fish monger's hand."

"Maybe he couldn't break into the safe." I suggested looking for the bright side.

"He broke into it alright and took everything with him but I will get my jewelry back I promise you that." Crystal said weeping.

"Play the tape I don't believe that he got in to the safe until I see it. It looks too tough to open without the combination," Suki said.

"Bullshit; Suki you just want see me to suffer."

"That's true Baroness but I want to see Chin that's a magic man at work he is unbelievable." Suki said excitedly.

Crystal's arm moved fast as a snake. She grabbed a letter opener from the side table and stuck the point in Suki's nostril and said.

"Just who is the magic man around here Suki Toyota? Should I take your nose Suki Toyota?"

"No don't Crystal you are the magic woman Baroness." Suki said childishly.

Crystal removed the paper opener and said. "I would have cut your nose off you know."

"I know Crystal; maybe we should all see our therapist." Suki said in a girlish voice.

"Yes, let's do that Suki. Let us tell them about the dead man under my bed." Crystal said hysterically.

"You look pretty relaxed Joseph do you have any idiotic ideas to add?" Crystal asked.

Blood started flowing slowly down her chin from her injured lips again. I took her in my arms. For a second she gave out a big sobs then she pushed me away gently.

She said. "Stupid Suki, is right, we have to see if he managed to open the safe."

She hugged Suki who melted in her arms in a little girls voice Suki cried. "You almost cut off my nose."

"Yes. Now lets go to the kitchen and see what that bastard left me." Crystal whispered.

We walked around the pool of blood gingerly and trooped to the kitchen. Suki spit on the pool of blood coming from Brown's body.

"Bastard! You gave us away. Rot in hell. If you needed money you could have asked the Baroness."

"I don't know if I would have given it to him Suki. A million dollars is a lot of money. I am not a gambler fifteen to twenty percent on my money was good enough. He probably knew that I never go for a million dollar bet on something as tricky as a pool game. The most I fronted him was hundred thousand dollars but I made it clear to him that was the limit.

Brown loved to pay back a debt. He usually had small bills and took his time counting it out. He was excited by money and I was caught up in his enthusiasm. He scored, because his cons worked. Tonight when Joseph hit Brown with the bottle I had a choice of saving Joseph and losing Brown, I made my choice I paid money to save Joseph. But I decided Brown would never get anything from me again not money, not favors nothing."

"You should have seen how out of control Brown was Suki. A mark hits him on the head which didn't hurt him at all. Instead punching Joseph in the face Brown pulled a gun. He almost shot Joseph right in my house mind you, right in my house. He was totally out of character. Now there he is dead under my bed. God! Hold me tight Joseph. I think I am going out of my mind."

I hugged her.

Suki grabbed my pants and said.

"I am not going out of my mind, Joseph but you can hug me anyway?"

Crystal let go and hissed.

"If this crap is not affecting you, how come your leg is trembling so hard, Suki Toyota? Hug her Joseph before she has seizure."

She climbed on to the bed and I hugged her. She was smaller than I thought. She pulled up her skirt no panties and rubbed against my crotch. I was totally aroused. Crystal poked me on my back and said.

"Joseph don't have sex right now. Save it for later. I never heard of a man who could resist Suki but there is this dead man under the bed and I have to see what is left in the safe."

I let go of Suki. She said with a full-lipped voice.

"You can whip my ass with a whip and leave it bleeding and I will still crawl back to you on my hand and knees, that hug will bring you big dividends Joseph."

To Crystal she said.

"I needed that hug Baroness. That creep under the bed is still playing with our sanity. See what's left in the safe and call the police.

"Ok, Suki but no police."

"What the hell do you mean no police?" Suki and I shouted together.

"What the hell are you going to with the body? How are you going to get the jewelry back?"

"No police! I am going to take care of this my way. Are you in Joseph?"

"I don't know what you plan to do Crystal. How can I be in on something that I know nothing about?"

"Remember you hit him with the bottle Joseph and I saved you." Crystal said pleading.

"I am in Crystal." I said really pissed.

"I am in too." Suki said giggling.

"No Suki. You go home and wait for my cell call. Your father still has the jet?"

"Yes, and why can't I go with you?" Suki said petulantly pursing her lips.

"Because you think with your vagina dear." Crystal said seriously.

"Of course I think with my vagina what other way is there? Why should that stop me from going along?" Suki asked getting mad.

"What if you fall for Big Chin. I bet you help him."

"That maybe the case in some situation, but not with Chin even though he is a magic man far as locks go. Didn't you see what was written on the back of his tee shirt Crystal?"

"No. What? I was too busy watching him rip me off."

The tee-shirt said.

"Besides fighting; I love sucking cock the best."

"There is no chance for me with a man like that. There is not a good bone in his body. I'll go home but not before I see what is left in the safe." Suki said dejected.

"What do you think of Chin, Joseph?" Crystal asked.

*A nasty customer, Chin is living a Taoist fantasy. He does what ever he wants until the accumulated negative energy will bring him down." I replied.

"I am going bring him down today. It is going to be the end of the road today, for Chin and his buddy Pool Hall Johnny." Crystal said as she opened the refrigerator door.

She had her pin keys out but she didn't lift the egg from egg tray instead she pulled out a bottle of champagne from the door compartment. She then stuck the key thin as needle into a hole right above the shelf. She stepped out of the way of the automatically dosing door. The fridge moved on its volition forward as far as it could then it turned right revealing the safe.

"There are five pin key holes in the fridge door. I never use the egg holder, because if an egg brakes it's hard to clean out the keyhole. Joseph did you catch how this system works? No! Well a thief comes in and if he is lucky he finds the keyhole. Once he has the keyhole and knows how to use it he has access to the old safe. Now the old safe is easy to break open and, because the thief will be satisfied with the couple million I leave there. I am really guarding my mother's jewels in the second safe behind this old one. A thief who finds hundred thousand dollars let alone three million will cut and run. He wouldn't bother searching for more. What do you think of the concept Joseph?" Crystal asked triumphantly.

"I think it's gorgeous set up but you got hit anyway. Who built this system for you?" I asked just to have her talk and calm down.

"Some Japanese guy I met in Amsterdam. He built safes for people with a lot of cash mostly dope dealers. He died suddenly when he went back to rob one of the safes he built. The guy who owned the safe added a switch that opened a door to a kennel of Dobermans, poor Hiroso, he was beyond recognition when they found him." chirped Crystal.

"That's great the guy is dead. He can't betray you." Suki said.

Suki and Crystal hugged and laughed.

"That's what I thought Suki. I was safe forever. But this Chin bum came along and ruined it all. Now I am going to open the safe so you two have to turn around." Crystal said.

We turned back when the sound of a motor started. The safe was going toward ceiling inch by inch.

"Can the safe fall?" I asked.

"No! The hydraulic system is tested for twenty tons." Crystal answered.

The second safe revealed was a beauty. The safe was made of stainless steel with two dials and a touch pad. We turned around so Crystal could open the safe. When the door was opened she gave out a loud scream.

"That bastard, I was hoping he couldn't open the safe but he did."

Her lips started bleeding again and she was sobbing so hard she was grasping for air. The safe was empty except for some papers. The safe must have held a lot of stuff because it was big as the refrigerator; shelf after empty shelf.

She turned to Suki and asked in a deep growling voice. "Where does Chin live?"

"I don't know Crystal. I never saw him before Brown made the bet. Why don't you call your foundation and let them take care of it. This is too big for you to handle by yourself." Suki said in a shaky voice.

"I can't the minute I call them everything becomes legal and I won't be able to get even with Mr. Chin. I am going to take his family jewels for pulling this shit on me. Didn't Chin tell Pool Hall Johnny to stay in the Good Luck Pool Hall for twenty four hours?" Crystal asked from no one special.

"Chin on the tape was pretty sure the Chinese Big Boss would not come for the money. I think we will find Johnny playing pool in Good Luck for at least the next twelve hours. He will know where Chin could by found. What time is it Joseph?" Crystal asked.

I was wondering where this was leading, "3:30 PM in the afternoon"

"Good, I am going to clean up and get dressed to kill for real." Crystal said still angry as hell.

Suki started laughing hysterically. I tapped her back with my palm lightly to stop her from flipping out. She turned around then jumped on me. Her feet wrapped around my waist she was light and smelled sweet, her hands grasped the back of my neck. Her leather skirt slipped up revealing her triangle of nakedness as she cried.

"Do me now Joseph right here on the floor."

She was grinding herself against me. I was overwhelmed with desire. I said.

"Yes it lets do it."

Crystal came in from the kitchen dressed in loosely fitting, candy blue, jogging clothes and square heeled shoes. She made a big thing of putting Brown's gun that had a silencer on it in her large purse.

She said. "Suki Toyota if you don't stop playing with Joseph until this situation is over I am going to lay you out next to Brown. Go home. Wait for my call. Get the plane ready and for goodness sake play with yourself instead of going after the first guy you see when you leave here, Joseph and I will have to move fast."

"Why can't I come along?" Suki asked striking a pose and pursing her lips.

"Suki darling the minute you are threatened you join the other side, Big Chin is threatening just standing there. You may join him."

"No, I wouldn't but I will go and why don't you use your corporate jet, Crystal?"

Suki asked with an unsure voice.

"I leased it for six months. It brings money in instead of costing a fortune just sitting there on the tarmac. I never use it." Crystal said itching to go.

"Penny wise and a pound foolish, I still think calling your foundation to take care of this situation is the best bet. They have the muscle to hush things up." Suki said.

Suki had the right idea but I realized there was no use talking to Crystal. She looked calm and collected but her eyes were crazed. I figured I would hang out with her to see how far she would take this thing.

Before Suki left Crystal and I went into the kitchen. Crystal moved the microwave oven to the side then she used her needle key on the wall to open a little cabinet that contained four three quarter inch tape machines. She emptied all the machines and replaced them with fresh tape. From one of the drawers she pulled some pre-stamped and addressed envelopes. I caught a glimpse of the address; Coconut Foundation in Netherlands. She pulled out a little drawer under the shelf supporting the tape machines; it contained packets of hundred dollar bills. She counted fifty thousand and handed it to me.

"That should be enough for us if we have to leave New York with or without getting my money and jewels back." Crystal said.

"Crystal I have a business here. I can't just get up and leave." I said.

"Yes you can Joseph. You must have someone in the office who can take over, what happens when you get sick? I will die without you Joseph. I need your strength behind me. Suki is a leaf blowing in the wind. I can't rely on her for anything. But you are like a deep well full of life giving water, you quench my thirst and give me strength." Crystal said looking pitiful with her lips swollen.

"Oh hell, Crystal I haven't had a vacation in years. I'll go with you but a week at the most. I'll call my brother. He will have a fit. I also have to drop my Palm Pilot off at the office it has passwords for my client's files. The office is on Fiftieth near Broadway. It's on the way to Chinatown, it should delay us no more than ten minutes." I said.

I had no place to go anyway. Ursula had the house. I could have asked my brother to put me up but he has four kids under ten, I would be in the way in no time. That left the Hilton, going with Crystal looked a hell of lot better.

Crystal gave me a peck on my lips. She left the taste of blood on it. She winced her lips were tender.

"Lets hurry up, I want to talk to Pool Hall Johnny badly. He is going to tell me where I can find Chin. It is too bad Suki does not know where Chin worked." Crystal said with a hiss.

"Did Brown ever tell you Suki where Pool Hall Johnny hangs out?" I asked.

"Yes it's on Canal Street. Good Luck Pool Hall is on the second floor of an old sewing factory. Suki said. "You could fire a cannon in the pool hall without anyone hearing it on the street. I was there when all this crap went down." Suki kissed me and Crystal and split.

I called my brother on the cell phone. He was pissed, because I did not show up for work in the first place and now when he heard that I was taking a week off without notice made him really mad. I told him I had problems with Ursula without going into details. I told him I would arrive in the office in ten minutes with the Palm Pilot. Robert was furious. Listening to Robert's rage on the phone I knew I was in for a long fight if we met face to face. When my brother starts ranting it lasts for hours I did not have an hour. I decided to drop the Palm Pilot off with the doorman avoiding the confrontation.

"I want to drop the tapes off at the Thirty Fourth Street Post Office. I want them delivered by tomorrow," Crystal said happily now that we started moving.

"Ok, I hope it's not crowded," I said worrying about the time. Pool hall Johnny might split from the Pool Hall.

"It won't take to much time the Express Mail boxes are pre-stamped. All I have to do is drop them in the mail box." Crystal murmured.

Crystal went to a shelf behind one of the mirrors and came back with a box that contained a gun that was a duplicate of Brown's silver plated gun. The box also held a silencer and ten loaded magazines.

"Here you take the gun Joseph," Crystal said with the crazy look in her eyes.

I reached for the gun but changed my mind.

"No, Crystal I don't need a gun. I have a firm belief if you pull a weapon you better be ready to kill, I am not ready to kill anybody."

"I am ready to kill so I will hold onto both guns." Crystal said as she emptied the contents of the box in her cloth Lord and Taylor shopping bag.

Crystal walked over to the bed looked down on Brown's body then said.

"You stupid little man you could have come to me before you made the bet and none of this would have happened but you chose to sell me out. A bum is always a bum. How many times did you tell me that Brown? You were a fricking bum when I met you and you left life as a fricking bum."

A trickle of blood started down her chin from her lips again.

"Let's get out of here Crystal it's four p.m. We may miss Pool Hall Johnny if we don't hurry up." I said

Crystal wiped her lips and applied lipstick then she said in a dull voice. "Ok, let's go."

We were half way down the stairway when a horrible thought struck me. I didn't know who had the tape that recorded the fight between Brown and me. If the cops found that tape I could be blamed for Brown's murder. The police could say I came back and shot him. It would be a nice frame.

"Crystal! Where is the tape from the machine you and Brown used for blackmailing the suckers?" I asked with a worried voice.

"It's in the VCR Brown wanted to take it but I told him twenty thousand dollars bought the tape not just your life Joseph. Wait, Wait Joseph, I had the tape with me when I went back to the club. I put it behind the counter with bunch of junk we never use. Are you satisfied?"

"No! I want that tape. I am going to destroy it. Let's go to the club first." I said with anger in my voice.

I was about to explain why I wanted to destroy the tape but Crystal shushed me, "don't say anything let me guess."

"You think if the cops view the tape they will think you came back after I left the apartment and killed Brown."

"Yes," I said not too happily.

"And of course like a good murderer you used two different guns to kill him, right Joseph." Crystal said with a tiny laugh.

"I don't care how much sense you are trying to make Crystal I still want that tape." I said.

She answered.

"OK and I hope Carmine does not have fifty million problems he wants to discuss with me, it's getting late."

We put the shopping bags full of express mail boxes containing the main surveillance tapes in the trunk of the car. We walked over to the club. Crystal asked Carmine to fetch the tape. When he did it I told him to put in the VCR and rewind it for a few seconds. The TV lit up with Brown facing the camera. I could see where the cut on his head was covered with a Band-Aid. Crystal reached over the bar and hit the stop button.

"I hope you are satisfied Joseph." Crystal said handing me the tape.

I took the tape without saying word as we walked to the car. I got on the West Side Highway the traffic wasn't too bad going south. I took the Fifty Seven Street exit and drove to the office. I couldn't find a parking place so I parked by a fire pump. I told her to move the car if a cop came. The wild look came back in her eye. I put my hand on her lips so she wouldn't bite them again. She was shivering like a gazelle.

I kissed her and told her.

"Relax, Crystal. I am coming back."

She stopped shivering and said.

"You better Joseph. Without you I'll fall apart."

I decided not to give the tape and Palm Pilot to the doorman too risky. Instead I rode the elevator to twelfth floor. I entered the Law and Accounting firm of Goodwin and Goodwin. In this normal environment it occurred to me that I was out my mind but I shook the feeling off, the hassle Crystal and I were in was real enough.

Barbara, our receptionist greeted me with a happy smile. I told her I was in a hurry and didn't have time to talk to my brother so would she give him my Palm Pilot. I told her to tell him to put the videotape in the safe without looking at it until I told him to do so. I asked her for an envelope and paper. I wrote the password that opened the file for all the other passwords on the Palm Pilot. I threw a kiss at Barbara and I was in the elevator.

I ran to the car where Crystal was dosing. It took longer then I expected to drive to the Post Office. I had to go around the building a couple of times before I found a parking place. She decided to send the tapes of Brown's murder by Registered Mail. The paper work held her up but finally we were on the way to Good Luck Pool hall on Canal Street in Chinatown. We made it in good time considering it was rush hour. I found a parking space just off Canal Street, good luck. The Pool Hall's windows one flight up faced Canal Street. However, the entrance was on the side street not too far from where I parked the car.

Crystal said.

"Here is the plan. When I say that's enough of your bullshit Johnny you grab him from behind pining his arms to his side. Joseph make sure to keep your knees together incase he tries to kick you in the balls with a backward kick. Hold him real tight while I talk to him about Chin and the jewelry."

"Ok, that's simple enough. I hope he is not too big." I said.

Looking across the street with surprise and anger Crystal hissed.

"What is Suki doing here? That bitch! That red Corvette is her car. When she is around things get weird. So get ready Joseph."

"When you two women are around things get weird for me." I whispered under my breath side stepping a wino who was sleeping in the street.

The stairwell leading to the pool hall was clean but dingy. We were about to climb the stairs when Suki came down from the opposite direction. She was dressed in red vinyl skirt and red blouse. She looked stunning.

"Suki Toyota what the hell are you doing here? You didn't tell them I was coming here did you?" Crystal asked in a hushed angry tone.

"No, Baroness I didn't tell anyone anything. I came to see the Boss. I wanted to rub his Ginseng until he satisfied me. That old man has a lot of KI energy that drives me wild for more and more. But there is nobody up there but your favorite person Pool Hall Johnny. I wanted him to abuse me a little bit but he is too afraid his wife might show up. I asked him where Brown was to just see him squirm."

"I knew it you had to stick your nose in it Suki. I bet you blew it. I think I am going to shoot you Suki Toyota." Crystal Interrupted reaching into her purse.

Suki sang in a whisper. "Om Om Om Om I am ready to die." She raised her left arm out as if she was on the cross. Her right hand raised her skirt to reveal her bush which released thin stream of urine. All the while she was singing one long Oooooommmmmm.

I had a fit of laughter.

Crystal said.

"Woman I can't believe you are real," looking around Crystal said. "We better keep our voices down Johnny might hear us before we are ready."

"Don't worry about him, he will stay up there until hell freezes over or when his wife comes for him. He is scared. His wife's grandfather made a big move against the Boss. But his hired assassin's failed him. They stabbed the Boss eight times but somehow the old guy survived. The Boss's faction rushed him to a hospital in Queens."

"He has support in the Queens' Chinese community. When the assassination failed most of the Chinese Men's Association pulled out of the fight waiting to see which way the coin fell. The betting is if Mr. Lu, Pool hall Johnny's wife's grandfather, survives the Boss's attacks from Queens he will be the next Boss. Mr. Lu's problem is a bunch of sixteen-year-old gangster boys in Queens who want to make a name for themselves by helping the Boss."

"So he is sticking close to his Mott Street house protected by hired Tong members. The invincibility of the present Boss is stronger away from the hubbub of Canal Street in Chinatown. Mr. Lu has the support of the Chinese Men's Association, because he succeeded in hitting the Boss's number one man Young Wong. With that move Mr. Lu got the Vietnamese Chinese gangsters to switch sides."

"Despite all the gunplay Lu thinks that at the end money will decide who will be the head of the Association. Mr. Lu knows the Boss does not have a pot to piss in. The Boss is a big time gambler. He shakes down businesses with special taxes to pay off personal gambling debts. He is unpopular among the New York City businessman. This episode with Brown was the final straw. On the other hand Mr. Lu's red envelopes with bribes are drawing him closer to the Chinese Men's Association in the city. He also hired Italian hit man from Little Italy to finish the Boss in Queens. Lu thinks they could slip in to the hospital dressed as doctors or janitors."

"How do you know all this Suki?" I asked.

"Johnny told me. I asked him where Brown went he said Brown went to Las Vegas. I didn't pursue the matter. I tried but he wouldn't play with me, because he was too scared that his wife might show up. Most man have bullshit excuses for sticking with their wives but this guy is up front about being pussy whipped."

"I asked him why the pool hall was so empty. He said the big fight was going in all the Chinatown's of New York, even in the suburbs. All the Chinese gunslingers were out fighting or protecting somebody. The fighting is so heavy that they forgot Johnny. Even the owner of the pool hall was out there toting a gun for Mr. Lu. In no time at all I got bored listening to fabulous Pool Hall Johnny. I don't mind listening to a man if some body action comes at the end of the conversation. But all Johnny could do is brag Mr. Lu this Mr. Lu that, a total bore.

"How come the police don't step in and stop the fighting?" I asked.

"Johnny said the red envelope with cash reached everybody. The cops won't interfere unless one of the young idiots shoots up a restaurant full of customers. Mr. Lu's men are fairly disciplined but some of the Boss's Queen's boys haven't handled a gun since their initiation into whatever gang they call home.

The boys may get nervous and shoot up a restaurant and kill some civilians. Mr. Lu wouldn't mind if that happened, because the Queen's branch of the Chinese Men's Association would drop the Boss like a hot potato and Lu would take over."

"I didn't like what I was hearing. I liked the Boss. I like a man who comes good and hard after getting his ass beaten by a bad little woman like me."

"There is nobody up there Suki?" Crystal asked incredulously. "What incredible luck Joseph." Crystal said patting my back gently.

"Yes only Johnny no one else. But didn't you hear what I said Crystal. There is a war going on. You play around here you may end up like Brown." Suki said intensely.

"I don't care who the hell becomes the head guy, the Boss, or Mr. Lu, I am not Chinese. All I want is my mother's jewelry collection back. I think everybody involved will understand. Did Johnny tell you where Chin lives Suki?"

Crystal's lips started bleeding again and she had that crazy look in her eye again. I whispered to myself.

"Man this is one weird trip."

"No Baroness he didn't tell me and I was too scared to bring it up. Johnny is dangerous too, because Mr. Lu expects to use the two million to recoup all the money he put in those pretty red envelopes to bribe the elders of the Men's Association." Suki said.

"Did Johnny actually say he had the two million?" I asked.

"No! Not like that, he just said he won some money and he was giving it Mr. Lu to fight the battle of the envelopes."

"You won't give it up will you Crystal?" Suki said with tears in her eyes.

"What's there too give up. He could keep the money but he has to tell me where to find Chin and the jewelry. I do have a problem Joseph. Johnny knows me. About five years ago a thief robbed my purse. He knocked me down to the sidewalk in the process. A valiant but short black man came to my rescue; Mr. Brown. He caught the culprit and Brown beat the thief up and returned my purse. We went to a bar and had a few drinks and we became great friends. I made him rich by lending him money at twenty percent interest. With that he could play his wonderful con games for last five years. When I saw Pool Hall Johnny on the tape, robbing my house, I almost threw up. My shinning knight in black armor turned out to be a turd. Those two sons of bitches ran a five year scam on me. Johnny was the thief."

Her eyes were crossing and she was shivering.

"Baroness, Brown didn't understand that it was your hand that was guiding him and making him rich and famous. The more you helped him the brighter he thought he was. He became so smart that he and Johnny decided to pull the big one and it spun out of control. Instead of sitting down and thinking things out when they were under the gun he and Johnny reverted to the two bit rats that you met five years ago. They sold you out. I never liked Brown. I never trust a man who won't give a woman what she craves; some old fashioned cum." Suki said.

Suki was really nervous. She was walking backwards and looking around for someway out of there as she was talking. I thought she would take a cab. Probably not a cab she had her Corvette parked couple of steps away, she just wanted fly.

"Suki don't you want to leave?" Crystal asked detachedly.

"I do and I am," Suki said.

She turned and showed me her panty less ass and said.

"If you survive this Joseph you beat me good for being such a coward."

Then she was gone with a last parting shot.

"Call me if you want the plane Crystal, dad has one in town," Crystal and I were left in the Good Luck Pool Hall's stairwell.

"I can't go up there. Johnny will attack me soon as he sees me. You have to go up there first and grab him." Crystal said.

"Me? What makes you think he won't attack me before I get to him? He knows Lu hired Italians to hit the Boss. He might think I am an Italian working for the Boss coming to kill him."

I was pissed like every soldier who had storm out of the trenches.

"Joseph go up there and when you enter the door holler that you are Detective Goodwin with a message from Mr. Lu. Show him your wallet but put it away before you get close to him. Walk over to him with confidence and grab him. Brown used to tell me that cops always spooked him no matter how clean he looked. Johnny is no different, he won't pull a gun on a cop. He is short as Brown and skinny. Try to grab him from behind and pin his hands below his elbow and watch out for kicks, keep your legs together against kicks. Soon as you got him I'll run over and cover him with Brown's gun. Hopefully seeing Brown's shiny gun will take the fight out of him. If not I'll . . ."

I interrupted her "Why don't we wait to decide what you will do to him until we get him. It's a good plan and I think I can carry it out if I don't wet my pants like Suki." I said shaking with anticipation.

Crystal became real excited. I don't think she expected that it would be that easy to convince me but to tell the truth I wanted the whole thing to be over and the plan was simple and reasonable. I walked up the stairs went trough the door announced that I was Detective Goodwin and I had a massage from Mr. Lu. Halfway there I flashed my wallet then put it away without him seeing a thing. Johnny was dumbfounded. He stood there with his mouth hanging open. When I reached him I said.

"Mr. Lu says Queen's collapsed."

He relaxed and started smiling. I grabbed him and spun him around. I pinned his arms to his side and applied the Heimlich Maneuver knocking the wind out of him. I held his diaphragm in place so he could not breathe. I let him suck in some air when Crystal arrived. She put Brown's gun to his head and said.

"I want the jewels back."

"Who the hell are you?" Johnny asked trying to shake me loose.

"Don't you remember me? You and Brown coned me five years ago with that bullshit purse snatching. I have been backing you and Brown ever since."

"Oh, it's you Crystal I haven't seen you in five years. You look so much older, so sorry." Johnny said with a smirk.

Crystal was taken back. She pulled a mirror out of her shopping bag looked at herself and said.

"You are a lying bastard Pool Hall I don't look at all older. I have a little blood around the lips but that will heal but you Johnny will never recover from a bullet in your head. Where are my jewels?

"I don't know what you are talking about. I don't know anything about any jewels." Johnny said defiantly.

I saw Crystal was at a loss. Johnny had her figured. She wasn't going to shoot him her only lead to the jewels. I got sick of the bullshit and gave Johnny another Heimlich Maneuver and this time I held his diaphragm until he turned blue. When he fell limp in I let him breath. In a real low tone I whispered to him.

"Does this picture seem familiar? Chin shot Brown in the head and you put two bullets in Brown's chest. We have the whole murder taped from four different angles in living color."

"You got the wrong guy. I wasn't anywhere near Crystal's apartment and I haven't seen her in five years. I got a wife who makes my money man I got kids, I don't live the life anymore." Whined Johnny the pool hustler.

I said.

"I tell you what Johnny if you don't have two million dollars in that brown leather bag over there I will let you go and give you fifty thousand dollars I have in my pocket. However if I find the money in the bag I am going to choke you until you tell me where we could find Chin and the jewelry."

Johnny started fighting like the devil but I held on to him. The little bastard kicked my shin so hard I almost let him go. But at the end I won, because I was a lot taller and stronger. I smothered him until he was too tired to fight. Crystal placed Johnny's brown bag on the pool table watching Johnny all the while. She opened the bag and there were two packages of money each one had one million dollars printed on the wrapping. Crystal looked at Johnny triumphantly and said.

"You can keep the money Johnny just tell me where Chin and the jewels are to be found."

"I can't. He will kill me and my children if I reveal that he had the jewelry. He is a crazy guy."

Crystal reached into her shopping bag for her keys. She selected a long thin key.

"I use this pinhole key to open my safe and now I am going to open you with it Johnny. Will you tell me where my jewels are located?" Crystal asked in an icy tone.

"No! Hell no! I can't go up against Chin."

She walked up to Johnny and stuck the key into his left eye. She twirled the key a couple of times in his eyes socket and stepped back to admire her work. Johnny passed out. He became dead weight in my arms. I got eye matter all over my sleeve. Crystal's lips were bleeding again. Blood was running down her chin. I was in a nightmare and there was no way out.

Crystal marched over to the water fountain and brought back a cup of water. She poured the water over Johnny's head and slapped him a couple of times. He came to and fought my hold but he didn't have much strength left. Crystal went over to him and ran the pin key down his nose."

What will it be Johnny? Chin's address or I'll take your other eye."

"Ok, ok, ok take it easy I'll give you the address. It's Chin's Locksmith on Elisabeth and Houston."

"We shall see Johnny." Crystal said.

She removed Johnny's cell phone from his belt and dialed information. She talked to the operator for a few minutes then disconnected the cell phone.

"No such number, no such name, Johnny. Brown told me once never trust a con man, because he will con you with his last dying breath." Crystal said wiping her bloody chin on her blouse.

"OK, ok, ok this is the real address, AAA Security Systems on Avenue C between 9th and 10th Streets." Johnny said sobbing.

"What is the store's number?" I asked him.

"I don't know the number but if you go there you can't miss it. It's on the basement level and it has red and yellow sign 'AAA Security Systems and Locksmith.' It's a real big place. He monitors the Chinese Men's Association's Automatic Teller Machine business from there." Johnny said with renewed vigor.

"What kind of taping system does he have in the store?" I asked.

"Nothing! Just like here in the pool hall nothing. He does business in the store. Some times big quantities of heroin pass through there. No taping." Johnny said quite animated.

"You threw the big pool game didn't you Johnny? There is no way you could lose against a young girl like that. You lost for the Boss against Brown." Crystal said a little relaxed.

I held onto Johnny despite the fact that he was cooperating. I didn't trust the little son-of a-bitch one bit. My mood was getting worse. I was on the edge too long. I just wanted to get out of there and finish the job of getting the jewels.

"No, no, no, you got it all wrong Crystal. The Boss is a strange gambler he likes to win when it's up and up, because he is testing his luck and skill. You can't test your luck in a crooked game, you always win. He would never ask me to throw the game," Johnny said, whimpering.

"Bullshit Johnny! How come you didn't recognize the young girl you played? She was in the pool hall almost every day. You were close enough for them to tape you together by a spy camera. You must have known she was a good pool player. It was a setup against Brown, I don't give a damn what you say." Crystal said triumphantly.

"How, how, how do you know all this? Is Brown alive? No, no, no he can't be not after those three shots he took, even the devil couldn't come back after that. I'll tell you why I don't notice young or any kind of woman while I am in China town, because I have a jealous wife. A couple of years ago one of those schoolgirls got brave and came over to my table. She wanted learn how to do bank shots properly. This led to this and that and next thing I know she is giving me a blow job in the bathroom."

"This deal went on for a few days. The girl bragged about it to her friends and my wife heard it on the gossip train. She lost prestige to a teenager front of all her friends. On the fourth day of my tryst with this girl, my wife who was waiting in the shadows somewhere in the pool hall, materialized and hit me over the head with a cast iron skillet. With that blow she got her prestige back, big time. All the young girls admired her. When I went back to the pool hall some of the girls would be brave and try to talk to me but I ignored them. After a while it became a habit I just stopped seeing them. That's the story. I didn't double cross Brown." Johnny moaned.

"The story is weird enough to be true but we con artist specialize in weird stories that ring true. Just the right amount of weirdness hooks the imagination of the sucker." Crystal said as she dialed the phone for information.

She talked for a couple of minutes and came back to Johnny, she put her face close to his and said.

"It is the right number and place Johnny. Remember this Johnny, I have tapes of Brown's murder. The tapes are out of my hand in a safe place.

If you have any ideas about getting even with me I will produce the tapes and you will go to jail for the rest of your life for Brown's murder, your wife will love that." Crystal screamed on top of her lungs.

"Ok, ok, ok I got the message you are a though bitch while this guy holding me." Johnny said with a smirk.

Crystal's arm moved lighting fast and stuck the needle key in Johnny's other eye.

"We will see how smart you are walking with a white cane." Crystal said pleased with her work.

Johnny passed out again. I dropped him to the floor and showed him under the pool table. He didn't move. I wondered if he was dead from shock. I went to the water fountain and washed off his eyeballs from my hands. I just wanted to get the hell out of there before his wife showed up.

I left the pool hall carrying Crystal's canvas shopping bag with the guns and Crystal carried Johnny's bag with the money in it. When we got in my car Crystal started telling me the direction I should take.

"I am not going." I told her.

Crystal with a calm voice asked.

"Why not Joseph?"

"We are going in to his lair. He has the advantage and this guy doesn't sound like he will fall for the cop routine."

I want to do is talk to him. I will give him all the money we got from Johnny for my jewelry that's pretty reasonable isn't it?" Crystal asked with a plaintive voice.

"Don't you realize Chin has to kill you?" I said

"Why does he? I'll offer him two extra million." Crystal asked.

"He will take the money and kill both of us. This type of guy will never allow us to live, because we know he killed Brown. He allowed Johnny a witness to live, because they were both on the job for the Boss. The only solution is to call the cops and let them take over." I told Crystal matter-of-factly.

"There is no way I am going to the cops. I will take a chance on getting killed before I go to the cops Joseph. All I need is for you to back me up, to be there. Joseph I am not belittling you with this offer but if you come with me I will give you the three million dollars these men took from me. Only thing I want is the jewelry." Crystal said with hope in her voice.

I put the key in the ignition and started the car.

"Yes, I'll do it." I said with my voice full of joy.

"What about getting killed Joseph?" She teased with a gentle laugh.

Driving there a little song was going around in my brain. Three million dollars in cash, Wow, I cleared a hundred thousand dollars after taxes last year. At that rate it would take me thirty years to make three million dollars. Wow! Three million dollars if I don't get killed. The thought of getting killed sobered me up. I asked Crystal.

"Do you have Chin's telephone number? I am going to give him a call. I want to know if the store is still open. Look around for a public phone booth Crystal. I don't want him to know my cell number. If he is in the store I will tell him I want a security system installed in my office. We'll see where we go from there."

I found a phone booth that had a working phone. I called the store. A woman answered. I asked her what the store's hours were. She said it was eight a.m. to nine p.m. I asked if Mr. Chin was in the store. She wanted to know why, I told her I was just opening a store on Broadway and I wanted a complete surveillance system installed. She wanted to know where I heard of AAA Security, I told her one of my Chinese contractors mentioned Chin's name. He said Mr. Chin's work was top quality and his prices were reasonable.

Her questioning and no answers pissed me off. I told her sharply do you guys want my business or not. She told me AAA Security wanted the business but Mr. Chin was out however, she could make an appointment for tomorrow around 12:30. I said Ok, I told her my name is Sol Steiner and I will call their company around twelve next day. What luck, Chin was out.

I went back to the car happy, I told Crystal the good news. She frowned and said.

"He's probably out there strong arming people for Mr. Lu."

"Why do you think he works for Lu?" I asked just to be contrary.

"Because, my lovely Joseph, Chin would never allow Johnny to walk away with two million bucks if he worked for the Boss." Crystal said with humor in her voice.

We drove to the store on Avenue C. I found a parking place after going around the block three times on Tenth Street. It wasn't a going to be a fast get away if something went wrong.

I told Crystal to go in first and ask the girl for direction to some restaurant. While the woman talked she could look around see how many employees there were in the store. I figured if there were only two or three people we could get the drop on them if we moved fast. Crystal balked. I asked her what was wrong.

She said petulantly.

"I don't want to be the heavy anymore. You have to start carrying a gun too Joseph, if you know how to shoot?"

"I can shoot a gun Crystal. I was a captain in the Army Reserve. We were issued side arms. You can relax I'll take one of those guns and lead the attack." I said with mirth in my voice.

Crystal rummaged in the canvas bag and handed me Brown's silver plated pistol and took its double for herself. The length of the gun with the silencer on it was awkward, because it didn't fit into my suit pocket. I showed it into my pants. I was hoping I wouldn't shoot my dick off when I pulled out the gun.

Crystal was in the store for quite a long time. When she came out she said.

"The woman is alone in the store. We talked a bit. She is quite nice. Taking her will be easy. There is an office in the back. If the jewelry is in the store it should be in the back office. I didn't see a safe up front."

"Ok, lets go." I said impatiently. The adrenal rush was burning my body. Johnny was right about the store, it was long. At the end of the isle there was a door with the legend, office employees only."

I walked over to the young Chinese woman and pulled out the gun. She didn't look frightened. I told her to go to the back office. She said the office was locked and her boss had the key. I told her to go to the office again. She said no. I was flustered for a moment. Crystal took over she went over to the girl and hit her on the shoulder with the butt of her gun. She said.

"Get over there and open the door or I will shoot you where you're standing. I have a silencer on the gun."

The girl led the way to the door which was open. It was wall to wall with electronic equipment. Next to a computer workstation there were three black garbage bags. On a little table next to the computer desk there was a diamond necklace. Half the diamonds were removed from the setting. Crystal picked up the necklace and said wistfully.

"This piece is from Queen Elizabeth the First's collection. It took my mother and her Black Corporation five years of planning to steal it. And this Chin moron is taking it apart. With these jewels the whole is worth a hell of a lot more than the parts. A quarter of my mother's collection is stolen. That's the reason why I can't go to the police. I had to recover them myself Joseph."

"Let's get out of here." I said totally flabbergasted by what I just heard.

I pointed my gun at the girl who was inching her way out of the office and said.

"You come here. Where are the handcuffs?"

"There are no handcuffs in store prick." She said defiantly with a liquid English accent.

I grabbed her by the hair and said menacingly. "Where the hell are the handcuffs?"

She stopped being smart and showed me the metal file drawer where they kept all sorts of police equipment including guns and duct tape and to my surprise the third million dollar pkg. I took the girl to the bathroom and handcuffed her to a steam pipe and put duct tape on her mouth. She got real mad and kicked my shin before I was out of range, it hurt like hell.

Crystal checked out the bags. It looked like everything they robbed was still in the bags. I grabbed two garbage bags. Crystal picked up the remaining bag. I put the million dollars in an AAA Security shopping bag that Crystal carried. She also wanted to take a gun that was in the file drawer. I told her not to do it, because the gun she picked up might be the one that killed Brown. She bitched but she put the gun back. She was like a pack rat every time she saw a gun she wanted to take it. We went back to the car without running into Chin.

We stowed the garbage bags and the canvas bag with the guns in the trunk of the car. I put the shopping bag containing the million dollars on the floor in the back seat next to the money we got from Johnny, all the money was mine.

I had to put the gun I was carrying under my seat I couldn't sit down with the silencer poking me in the groin. Things were real cool but I had no idea what to do next. We couldn't stay at Crystal's apartment so, the best bet was to go to a hotel. I decided to go to the Chelsea Hotel on Twenty Third Street an old hotel but it had atmosphere. Crystal fell asleep soon as we got in the car. I tried waking her to get Suki's cell number but she was dead to the world.

I drove on to Ave C not thinking of anything just numb from tiredness when a van behind me bumped me; nothing heavy just a light bump. I looked in my rear view mirror and to my shock there was a brown van with the legend "Emergency Locksmith," written on the hood. I jumped the red light and made a left turn then when I came to Avenue D, I made another left. The van was right behind me as I made the left. To my shock I was in a dead end street. A big Chinese man climbed out of the van, ponderously, as if he had all the time in the world. A red car, that I didn't notice earlier, pulled in front of my car; I was boxed in. Meanwhile, I was desperately searching for my gun under the seat. I couldn't find it. The gun must have slipped toward the back out of reach. Chin came over to the car and shouted.

"Get the hell out of the car or I'll break every fricking bone in your body before I'll kill you."

While Chin was hollering two guys came out of the red car in front of me. One the men was carrying sawed off shotgun the other one a small machine gun. Chin shouted at them to hold off shooting until he dragged me out of the car. He punched the window, it rocked the car. The window held but not for long if he kept punching it. One of the guys from the red car called to Chin. He turned toward them shouting.

"I said wait until—"

A shotgun blast tore half of Chin's face off. The second blast took off top of his head. Two short burst of the machine gun and he fell over like a giant redwood. The two Chinese men from the red car swaggered over to the body and said to it.

"You were wrong to think that the Gold Chinese Dragon's of Vietnam would sell out the Boss. We took your money Chin and pissed it away on wine and women while we were waiting for the orders to blow you away.

"As for you two," one of the Gold Dragon's said.

"The Boss says what you did to Johnny broke Mr. Lu's will to do more harm. Mr. Lu thought the Boss did it. Mr. Lu wants to negotiate. Our killing of Mr. Chin, Mr. Lu's toughest supporter, was the Boss's answer to negotiation. The Boss says you are welcome to Chinatown anytime. Before the pair left I told them, "I don't know if you heard but Mr. Lu hired some Italian gun man from Little Italy to pose as doctors or janitors who will go to the hospital to hit the Boss."

Both guys laughed and said.

"That's Chin's doing. We will see how Mr. Lu does without Mr. Chin's strong arm. How come you like the Boss?"

"We have a friend who really likes the Boss. So we like the Boss too. We trust her judgment." I said with good humor, happy to be alive.

"That must be Suki. We like Suki too. We never met anybody so crazy. Too high class for us though." They said it, laughing, and then they ran to their car and left burning rubber.

I followed them out real fast. I turned on to the Avenue and gunned it. Soon I was on Canal heading for the FDR drive. I was worried about cops but there were no sirens, nothing. Thank God it was that type of neighborhood where people waited for a while before they called the cops.

"Are we safe and alive?" asked Crystal in a small voice. I think I peed in my panties when that shotgun went off. I thought it was you who got shot and I was next. I am still afraid to open my eyes." She said crying.

"Things were happening too fast for me to get scared, that is until Chin hit the car window then I was scared. Seeing him get killed was pure pleasure." I said happily.

I was worried about riding around in this car. We were sunk if somebody copied the license plate numbers and gave it to the cops. I was also sleepy and hungry, we had go to the hotel and sort things out. Crystal was almost catatonic. I gave her a kiss on the forehead. She came out of it.

"We don't have too go to the Chelsea. Suki has an apartment on Park Ave. and Sixtieth. I have the keys I could use it anytime. The doorman will park the car at a nearby garage." Crystal said sobbing.

Park Avenue? These women are super rich. And now in a small way so was I. I have the three million dollars that I earned, the rough way. I drove off the FDR and headed for Park Avenue and Sixtieth Street. When we arrived Crystal jumped out of the car and called to the doorman. They returned with a luggage cart. She loaded the three garbage bags full of jewelry on the cart and also the brown bag with two million dollars in it. She carried the canvas shopping bag with the guns. I carried the shopping bag with the million dollars we recovered from Chin. I also had to get my gun. I told them to go ahead, I would catch up with them. I found the gun under seat stuck in the webbing of the seat. I put the gun in my waist. They were waiting at the elevator. The doorman looked stoic. Crystal was impatient, Crystal said.

"Joseph give your car keys to Charles. He will park the car in the long term parking garage."

"How long?" I asked unprepared.

"I thought six months is about right. I already gave him a check for three thousand dollars." Crystal said just barely holding anger out of her voice.

I dug out my key chain and removed one of the car keys and handed it to Charles, reluctantly. I didn't have time to think over the implication of giving up my wife's car. Ursula may report the car stolen. Hopefully, she and Jack West were so into each other that worrying about her car and me would be too much of a bother; she had my Mercedes anyway. James and I walked back to the car. He got in on the driver's side as I searched the glove compartment. I didn't find anything important.

I let James to go ahead and park the car. I walked back into the lobby.

Crystal was jittery. When we got off the elevator I asked her what was wrong.

"Nothing! You should have shot Chin." She said with a hiss in my ear.

"With what gun? Mine was under the seat stuck in the webbing."

"Why was it under the seat?" She asked.

"The silencer on the gun was so long I couldn't sit down without the damn thing hurting my balls." I replied angrily.

We got off on the fourth floor. There was one door on the floor. A three-dimensional dragon covered the door. The doorframe was made of bamboo. The whole effect was pure Suki, gaudy to the nth degree. Crystal opened the door grumbling to herself.

We rolled the valet cart into the apartment. Crystal became a nasty guide. She spit out the words.

"The first room to the left is decorated with museum quality Italian furnishing worth a king's ransom. The second room is museum quality Chinese furnishing worth millions. The third room is early American and has a fortune in Shaker furniture. I really like that."

On the right there was only one door but it was big. Crystal stopped rolling the cart and opened the door. I found myself in a castle. There was a long roughly honed table and wooden chairs around it. Windows were stained glass. The walls were made of square blocks of stone. The floor was mosaic tile depicting a medieval hunt. Straight ahead there was another door that led to an ultra modern kitchen big enough to feed a hundred people.

"Suki's father liked a castle in Scotland. He hired a decorator who worked as a set designer for Disney. He gave him Cart-Blanche. Francois Frishy, his designer, came up with this monstrosity. Suki's father loves it. Not a bad place to have parties; you can sit sixty people at the table and forty under it."

I cracked up laughing.

"I didn't mean it to be funny Joseph." Crystal said in a totally bitchy voice.

"Sorry to laugh but you are funny Crystal. This is some apartment." I said.

"It's just beginning." Crystal said not mollified.

We reached a hallway. She said.

"If you go down the left side of this hallway then turn right you will find eight bedrooms usually used by guest. If you go down the right side of the hallway and then turn right you will find six rooms reserved for the servants. I have not decided which side of the hallway you will occupy Joseph."

I didn't say anything in return but I couldn't laugh off that nasty cut. I also couldn't figure out what was wrong with her. She had her victory. Chin is dead. She had her jewelry. She should be jubilant. It was probably the let down from all the pressure we were under. She opened a door on the far wall of the hallway. Warm humid air came wafting out inviting me in. It was a large room. In the center of the room there was a pool made of salmon colored tiles. The pool must have been eighteen by twenty feet long and four feet deep.

There were potted plants in giant pots on the floor and orchids, wild flowers and fern pots covered the walls. The room was marvel to behold. Crystal doing her guide routine said her voice a bit more relaxed.

"Suki's father thought he would introduce the Japanese bath custom to his American associates so he had this pool built. It never really worked. The American male executives went along with the nudity but the female executives balked. The pool caused disharmony; a big taboo for a Japanese executive in those days. He dumped the apartment on his daughter Suki. He seldom comes here. The door on the north wall leads to Suki's bedroom. The two doors on the west wall lead to Mr. and Mrs. Toyota's rooms. The room on the east wall is mine."

"What is holding up the floor? The water must weigh a ton." I asked hoping to receive a civilized answer.

"You hit their problem on the head. They had to reinforce the floor from below. At the time I happened to own the apartment below. He made me an offer I did not want to refuse.

A lot of cash plus a ninety-nine year lease for a six-room apartment in the artiest section of Tokyo, the district is alive day and night. I met Suki again when I went to Japan to see the property that she sold me, she was the wildest and sharpest woman I ever met. Except when her Daddy or Mommy are around then she is the young bumbling Japanese scholar."

"Where the hell is she anyway?" I asked.

"She must not be coming here, usually before she comes to this apartment she calls her servants, giving them four hour notice to get the place together. I don't see any servants."

As she was talking she was rolling the cart toward her room. I grabbed it and held it back.

"What are you going to do with the stuff?" I asked my suspicion rising.

"Not that it's any of your business but if you must know I am putting it in a safe." Crystal said sarcastically.

"Will you give me the combination for the safe?" I asked calmly.

"No! Why the hell should I?" Crystal said furiously.

I didn't say anything her but I did remove Johnny's brown bag with the two million dollars and the AAA Security shopping bag with Chin's million dollars from the valet cart. The bitch pulled a gun from her canvas shopping bag and pointed it at my chest.

"You don't deserve the three million. You didn't shoot Chin. You put our life in danger." Crystal said with clenched teeth.

"You know something Crystal I am very happy I didn't shoot Chin. If we get caught they can only hold me for torturing Johnny and hitting that Chinese girl in Chin's shop. If you were to get caught you face the same charges heavy but not murder.

"That's all we did?"

She put the gun back in to the canvas bag."

"I feel like I killed six men."

I saw an evil spirit lift from her shoulder. She started laughing.

"I better get in the shower fast I haven't urinated in my panties since I was a very little girl. I am totally embarrassed. Take Mr. Toyota's room Joseph. As for the money, Joseph it is yours for keeps."

"There was no doubt about that." I said wickedly.

I took the brown bag and the shopping bag with the money and walked over to Mr. Toyota's room. I expected something Asian but it had a king size bed covered with a gold embroidered bedspread. The furniture was original art deco. Toyota must have liked Picasso, because there were three signed ones on the wall. I went into the bathroom.

clever. His guard was relaxed because Chin's death took the fight out of Mr. Lu. We all have to watch ourselves if Johnny comes out of his coma and tells his wife who we are. She might try to harm us also. She is insane with grief.

"So, Mr. Lu is the Boss now?" Crystal asked not at all disturb by what she heard.

Suki said that Lu was dead too. "The Vietnamese Chinese killed him. They got to him after they killed Chin. The war is over. You won't believe this but the new Boss is the old Boss's number one man, Young Wong."

"Young Wong caught wind of the alliance between Lu and Chin. He looked at the odds and decided the Boss might lose in a big way. He decided to die. He moved into a coffin in a Chinese funeral parlor until a trusted boy, who was a child of ten, told him to come out. There was a power vacuum and Young Wong was the man to fill it."

"The old men of the Chinese Men's Association' elected Young Wong the Boss without the usual fanfare, because after all the fighting they wanted a man who had as much brains as brawn."

"How do you know about Johnny's wife killing the boss? She would keep it a secret wouldn't she?" Crystal asked with disbelief.

"She is stupid cow. Look at her choice of men. Soon as she got back to the restaurant she started bragging to the women. In no time it was all over the Chinese women's gossip circuit. Her prestige among the women is in the stratosphere. Her name is Nancy by the way."

Di Di sat on the yellow tiled floor and said.

"You better not go to the funeral Suki. Nancy is going to be there to gloat. She might connect you to Boss; I mean the ex-Boss. You never know what a crazed woman will do."

"I don't think she will spend much time at the funeral. She has to bury her grand father and take care of her husband she should be busy for a while; shouldn't she?" Suki answered with doubt in her voice."

"Di Di interrupted. "I called Peter Wong's Inquiry Agency in London. I asked him to look into the gang situation in New York and to check whether there was any danger for you Suki. He just called and told me there was serious danger from Johnny's wife Nancy Lu but as you said Suki it was not immanent she has too many things to juggle right now. However, Cathy Chin is red hot for revenge. Losing her brother sent her over the edge. She tried to hire Vietnamese gunny boys to shoot you Suki and the two Americans you were seen with in the Pool Hall's entrance."

"Peter Wong called Young Wong the new Boss, they are relatives by-the-way, to put a stop to Cathy Chin's activities before she started another war. Young Wong called Ms. Chin personally. He told her if she wanted to continue the ATM business she better forget what happened during the war, no revenge, he wanted peace. She accepted the offer meekly." Di Di said with some doubt in her voice.

"You don't believe Cathy do you Di Di?" Suki and Crystal asked at the same time.

"No, but she won't do anything right now. She has to prove that she could run the business without her brother. There are plenty of smart guys in the Association who would love to take the business away from her. She has to watch her Ps and Qs. But if she mourns her brother too long it will fester. Sooner or later she will hunt for you and Crystal. By the way my calls to Peter Wong's cost your father twenty thousand pounds."

I said. "Cheap at the price."

Suki went over to Di Di and sat in her lap and hugged her with tears in her eyes then she said.

"Thank you, milk mother where is dad's next plane going?"

"Miami, Florida, it's carrying three complete heart, lung and liver transplants."

"When is it leaving?" Suki asked with a sigh.

"When they finish harvesting the body parts, you have plenty of time. I'll call the limo. It should get you to Kennedy airport in plenty of time."

"Witch!" Crystal addressed Di Di. "Are you going to let us on the airplane?"

"Yes and no. I just spent twenty thousand pounds for some very important service for the three of you. I would like to see six thousand six hundred pounds from you and Joseph and no weapons on the flight." Di Di said yawning.

I could see Crystal was going to argue. Suki, Di Di and I chimed in together.

"You are not getting on the plane with weapons these paranoid days, Crystal!"

"So, that's how it is. Well I am not going to be left behind, that is for sure." She whispered.

Crystal got up slowly letting me take a good look at her behind. Her eyes locked with mine and the heat between us was on again.

"There is the smell of fish in here. Crystal close your legs." Di Di smirked.

"You are just a jealous Witch, because I finally got a boyfriend. I am going to get my checkbook. Are you happy Di Di?"

Suki and Crystal left the bathroom giggling like high school girls.

"What about you Joseph? Are you going on the plane to Miami?" Di Di asked.

"Nobody asked me but if they do I will be happy to go." I was trying to be coy and independent front of Di Di.

I knew full well Crystal would not go without me. Suki would but she was a strange bird anyway. One minute she was all yours the next minute she was gone like the willow wisp.

"Well, I am asking you. The ticket price is six thousand six hundred pounds, English money and it's worth every penny. Cathy Chin has it in for you and Crystal. Young Wong has her boxed in by holding her business hostage. But you never know with women she might say screw the business and avenge her brother. Nothing we could do about that but we will get plenty of warning from the new Boss. Peter Wong guaranteed that for a hefty price of course. Are you going to fish or cut bait Joseph? Are you in or out?" Di Di asked forcefully.

"I am in!" I said.

Now if you don't mind I am going to get my checkbook and write you a check for eleven thousand dollars to cover the money you spent on Peter Wong. I was in the tub and she was sitting on the floor and from her demeanor I understood that she was going to wait until I got out of the bathtub. I said screw it I walked past her not covering anything. She looked me over real good and said.

"Not quite a stud but respectable." Di Di laughed.

I went back and kissed her on her forehead and thanked her for the compliment. She didn't resist she just rubbed my leg.

I went into the room assigned to me and looked under the bed. The brown bag and Chin's security shopping bag were there. There were three packages with a million in each next to them on the floor. I pulled on shorts and pealed off eleven thousand in hundreds. I took it back to Di Di who was cleaning the bathroom.

"No thank you Joseph I am paying with a check so I would like to be repaid with a check. Cash is a big pain in the ass in this country." Di Di said.

"Di Di, I just looked I don't have that much money in my checking account it's cash or nothing." I said.

"I know you don't have that much in your checking account. I checked your credit. But I just want to show you that cash can be a millstone around your neck, convert it soon as possible." She took the cash and pecked me on the lips and left.

I didn't think I had a problem. I had Crystal's contract, which made it legal but I didn't want to pay forty percent in taxes on it right now. I needed time to figure out the angles. It's going to be fun filling out my income tax return next year.

Suki came into the bathroom wearing a blue business suit and wide brimmed hat. She looked like the perfect socialite.

"If you don't close your mouth Joseph a fly will fly in it. It's my father's plane and he has dress rules on his planes. Di Di will press your suit but you will have to find a shirt and shorts in dad's closet. He keeps different size clothing for guest." Suki said.

"When are we leaving?" I asked.

Crystal came into bathroom. She was dressed in a yellow suit and a white blouse and a big sapphire encrusted with diamonds on her suit lapel.

"One of your mother's jewelry?" I asked.

"Yes. A Maharaja became quite wealthy when she bought it. What are you going to do with the money Joseph? They search bags at the airport even if you are going by private plane."

Suki said.

"You can leave it here."

I didn't want to hurt Suki's feeling but there was no way I would leave it in her apartment. If Suki got angry with me I would be out three million bucks. I was planning to rent a safe deposit box for the money but the banks were closed.

"I'll take it with me." I said.

"I don't think that's a good idea!" Suki and Crystal chimed together.

Di Di was watching from the door.

"Your suit is ready Joseph. You better hurry up. The plane is leaving in two hours."

"Ok, Di Di, how do we get the money on the plane?" I asked fear, anger and frustration showing in my voice.

"Did I say I saw a pair of perfectly matched diamond earnings on Forty Seventh Street." Di Di answered.

"It will be my pleasure to present it to you." I said.

"No, no that won't be necessary. I will buy it, five thousand should cover its cost." Di Di said smoothly.

It crossed my mind that I could stay in New York, but I said. "OK, I'll deduct it as expenses."

I went into my room to get five thousand dollars in hundred dollar bills. Di Di followed me into the room and whispered in my ear dramatically.

"There will be an extra box of Pharmaceuticals on the plane. The box will be delivered to you when you reach Miami."

"Where exactly are we staying in Miami?"

"Crystal owns a mansion in Coconut Grove and a Palace just outside Miami. She spoke to the servants. Everything will be ready when you arrive." Di Di answered like secretary.

I picked up the three packages of hundred dollar bills. I decided to trust her but there was a heavy feeling in the pit of my stomach. I pealed off ten thousand dollars and put it in my freshly pressed suit pocket. I patted the rest of the suit's pockets.

"Where is the fifty thousand dollars?" I asked suspiciously.

"Crystal took it. She said it was her money." Di Di said, clearly resenting that I mistrusted her.

"It is her money. Sorry Di Di, I didn't mean to jump on you. I'll wait for the package in Miami, thanks."

She gave me a card with her land line telephone, cell phone and fax number. She also wrote her address in the West Village on the back of the card and said.

"If you have any kind of trouble, no matter where you are, just call."

Crystal came in the room looking great in the yellow silk suit, the hem of the skirt bellow her knees, she said.

"Don't worry Witch we won't get into trouble. By the way my mom's Black Foundation will take care of Mr. Brown on Seventy Fourth Street. It's the first time I called them in a long time. They are very happy to help me."

"Did you call them to get action?" Di Di asked.

"Yeeees," said Crystal waiting for a trap.

"That's your problem you have this magnificent organization with you at the top. And no one comes to your aid unless you ask." Di Di criticized.

I called London for Suki before she even thought of asking me.

"The company wasn't like a pyramid when I first inherited it. There were thirty to forty people whose job was to see to my comfort. It was suffocating. I felt I was a prisoner. I separated myself from their loving kindness when I learned how to operate the Company." Crystal said proudly.

"You should have the Black Foundation clear the road for you instead of just cleaning up after you." Di Di said wisely.

"I'll think about those pearls of wisdom, but for right now, I will leave the situation the way it is." Crystal said with finality in her voice. By the way Di Di how would you like to make thirty thousand dollars?"

"I am listening." Di Di answered with intense interest.

"Pack the jewels in the garbage bags in boxes and take them to my Zurich Bank's branch office on Broadway. Here is the address." Crystal said handing Di Di a card.

"I'll do it for seventy thousand." Di Di said excitedly.

"We are in a rush Witch, I will give you fifty thousand and that's it."

"OK, cheapskate, fifty thousand it is."

"I am not cheap. I am frugal. Di Di you had better handle the jewels discreetly. Give them to the bank manager. He has instructions what to do with them but don't forget to get a receipt." Crystal growled.

"Don't worry Crystal I will take care of it. Give me a check now and you can be on your way my frugal lady." Di Di smiled like a cat that ate a bird.

Crystal took out her check book and wrote out the check and said.

"These jewels are costing me too much damn money. So far three million and eighty four thousand dollars, but I am taking care of them Mommy, your little Crystal is taking care of them." Crystal whispered with tears in her eyes.

"And how many people died over it? You must have a jewel with very bad luck on it," Di Di said mysteriously.

"You are not getting superstitious on me, are you Di Di?" Crystal asked alarmed.

"Don't worry Honey the fifty thousand is going to buy safety for your precious stones. Is it really true that you Mom robbed some of those jewels?"

"That is what I been trying to tell everybody. She was insane about famous jewelry. If a jewel was well known or unusual she had to have it. While Dad was alive she couldn't do much more than to offer big bucks but when he died she discovered the Black Foundation. Originally, the Black Foundation was Dad's industrial espionage arm.

Dad used the Blacks to attack and counter attack corporations who were trying to steal industrial secrets from him. Mom turned them into jewel thieves. Nobility all over the world is missing jewelry that they wouldn't sell to her. She had jewels, she wanted and could not buy, duplicated then the Blacks would do the switch. Sometimes if the jewel was just famous it cost her more to make the duplicate and run the operation than the original was worth on the open market. She had 'copy' inscribed with a laser on the duplicates. She managed to switch one of Elizabeth I of England's necklaces. It took five years of scheming for the Blacks to do the switch but they did it."

"How did she do that?" Di Di asked excitedly.

"They got to the assistant curator. He liked to use cocaine. The Black's created a game for him. Every time he bought drugs his connection would get arrested. It did not take long before the drug dealers put two and two together and took action.

They gave him a terrible beating but the busts continued every time he bought cocaine the dealer would get busted. One of the Black Foundation's woman made friends with him and became his lover. She had very good connections in the drug underworld and she would introduce him to new dealers when the old dealers dropped him like a hot potato. In England murder is highly unusual but one dealer whose gang got busted three times, because of the assistant curator had enough and ordered him murdered.

His girlfriend from the Black Foundation picked up the information and warned him. He could not go to the police, because it would get back to his royal employers. He would get fired plus he would be blacklisted in the art world. He had no talent for any other job.

The Black Foundation bought off the dealer who ordered the hit. They wanted the assistant curator alive and scared so they told the dealer to continue to spread the rumor that the assistant curator would be murdered by Christmas.

Black Foundation operatives followed the assistant curator openly everywhere he went. After two weeks of this treatment the assistant curator was a nervous wreck afraid to leave his house. His Black Foundation girlfriend told him that a very influential fence would buy off the drug dealer if he did a special job.

Once the little mouse understood which way the wind was blowing he was quite happy to do it. The curator was a very smart man. He realized that he was set up. He told his Black Foundation girlfriend whom he suspected was part of the plan that if they would have offered him a pound of cocaine he would have switched the necklace happily. The Black foundation put him on retainer, they like smart corruptible guys in important positions.

After five years of different games, my mother got the necklace within a week. My stupid, darling mother didn't keep records of her thefts and her real purchases. So the whole lot is tainted. I was planning to go trough her checkbooks to see what she bought legitimately but I never found time. And what bad luck that moron Chin comes and steals them. I had to get it back. Do you hear me Joseph?"

"Well it brought out a side of you nobody knew existed." Di Di said laughing.

"You had to be there to see the pure insanity of it all." Suki interjected as she was watching me get dressed,

"Yes! It was one hell of an experience. If you guys are ready to go I am too." I said.

"By the way Crystal why did you have to do the dirty work when you have the Black Foundation at your beck-and-call?" I asked.

"Because they over plan everything. You heard what that curator said, if they would have offered him a pound of cocaine, he would have switched the necklace happily. It took them five years to accomplish something that could have been done in a week. And the truth is that it took a lot of money and effort to buy off the dealer who wanted the assistant curator murdered. They had to set the guy up in Australia; the man wouldn't accept anything less. It was really tricky because the guy had a criminal record. They had to grease a lot of hands before the dealer was given residency.

I pensioned thirty people from the Black Foundation and kept the seven people who knew they worked for me when mom died. They will get rid of Brown's body but it will be too complicated and cost a fortune, as for anything complex they are short handed and slow."

Di Di clucked over us like a mother hen. She kissed Suki a dozen times. The women had carryon bags. I felt naked without one. Suki must have read my mind.

"Don't worry Joseph. We are going by private plane. No one will notice you don't have luggage."

I looked at my watch it was one a.m. It was something like thirty-six hours since Ursula and I split. Shit! I have been going through the changes. We got in the elevator, this time it had an elevator operator punching the buttons. A stretch limousine was waiting. An Asian driver opened the door bowing at the waist.

Suki returned a short bow of her head. Crystal ignored him and got in the car. I bowed at the waist. He bowed again. I was going to bow again but Suki grabbed my suit jacket and pulled me in the car. She said.

"Occidentals, don't have to bow."

"Not even to your parents?" Crystal asked wickedly.

"You better bow before my parents if they bow to you Joseph. Father usually shakes hands but among Japanese people he likes to keep things formal. Crystal if we run into my father behave yourself please. He still can't get over how you took him on the construction of the pool."

"A girl has to take care of herself." Crystal said laughing.

"How did she take you father?" I asked, happy to change the subject.

"My father bought the fourth floor of the building, you saw, for a reasonable price by Japanese standards but at an inflated price by American standards. He didn't care, he had an apartment on famous Park Avenue. The only thing the apartment lacked was a pool. He called in a Japanese Company that specializes in building indoor pools. The company's engineers told him that it was possible to build the pool but some of the support beams would have to be strengthened on the third floor. Nothing major but it would increase the support for the pool, water is very heavy."

"Let me guess. Crystal owned the third floor." I said laughing.

"Yes." Suki said. "And it's not that funny Joseph when you are on the receiving end. My poor father went down to see his downstairs neighbor. Crystal's youth threw him a curve she couldn't have been more than twenty eight years old. Crystal's butler served father good Japanese Sake and sandwiches.

The Sake broke the ice very nicely. Before my father knew it he was pretty tipsy. He told Crystal of his plans to install a pool on the fourth floor but some of supporting beams had to be strengthened in her apartment. She told him he could do what ever he wanted. My father was very happy to get what he thought was an agreement.

Poor father, he was so tipsy he didn't really pay attention to Crystal's careful noncommittal words. He taped the conversation but he didn't listen to tape until it was too late. The pool is fiberglass. It was hoisted into the fourth floor through one of the windows in four pieces by a crane. The plan was to finish the job really fast. While the fiberglass pool was being assembled another crew would work in Crystal's apartment reinforcing the support beams. The whole job was meant to take a week and cost fifty thousand dollars."

"Here is where they put me into a bad light." Crystal interrupted. "But what's missing from Suki's rendition of what happened, compensation. I was also worried about a leak. Their engineer pulled out plans and charts to prove how safe the pool would be if I allowed them to reinforce support beams in my apartment."

"As I listened to this guy talk about plumbing I realized they were at a total disadvantage. I was brutal. I told Mr. Toyota that I couldn't accept anything less than two million dollars or buy the third floor at a hefty price more than the market value."

"I thought he was going to have a stroke he turned so red. He offered fifty thousand that I refused. After a while he calmed down and took a long look at me as if he saw me for the first time and said."

"You are very young are you not? I am going to send my daughter over tomorrow. You two can work out a deal. However, buying your apartment is out of the question Crystal."

"He took my hand kissed it and left. I haven't seen him since than. But the next day an off day for my help the bell rang and I answered the door personally. There were these two persons standing there. A Japanese young woman who was dressed to kill, she wore a tight lemon yellow skirt that barely covered her underwear, she wore a translucent blouse that revealed a yellow bra, her shoes were extra high yellow leather platforms. She struck a pose and said.

"I am Suki Toyota and this is Di Di Sugaro my milk mother. What's up? My father is blowing a gasket. This is the first time he asked me to conclude a business deal for him. I don't know where to start."

"How about inviting us in the apartment for starters." Di Di said in her heavy Irish brogue as she pushed passed me.

"Where is the Butler?" She asked in that Irish accent. Di Di was dressed in a Kimono, her hair had a big bun, held together by pins. Only thing jarred her classic appearance was a pair of large red platform athletic shoes.

"The staff is off. If you had called I would have had someone here. Sooo, if you come back another day." I said to get them out.

"You are really an infant, aren't you? There are twenty construction workers upstairs doing nothing but farthing all day. I hope I didn't hurt you gentle ears by using the 'farthing' word dear." Di Di replied looking around.

"Thanks for the insults. It is not a bad thing to do when you want something nice from a person and yes I prefer the term passing gas." Crystal said, leading them to the living room. A rude sound came from Di Di's direction.

Adjusting her Kimono Di Di said. *"Sorry! I passed gas."*

Crystal looked at Suki and Suki looked at Di Di and suddenly all three cracked up in uncontrollable laughter.

"Sake?" Crystal asked.

"I'll have Irish whiskey and bring the bottle." Di Di replied. *"I'll have Pink Gin."* Suki said shyly.

"I don't think we have Pink Gin but we will when you come the next time."

"Then I'll have Tequila straight."

"What will you have?" asked Di Di pouring a drinking glass full of whiskey.

"Screwdrivers, I always have a pitcher full for unexpected company." Crystal said pointedly.

In a half hour the whole company was roaring drunk, Di Di fished a big bundle of papers from her purse and said.

"Suki and I don't care if you sign this contract or not, but her father is frantic."

"He couldn't be too frantic if he is not paying the two million." Crystal said slurring her words slightly.

"Mr. Toyota thinks money doesn't mean much to you. So, he'll make a deal that you might like. He has a six bedroom apartment in the theatre district of Tokyo He is willing to lease it to you for ten years free of charge."

"If I do it has to be a ninety-nine year lease and seventy five thousand dollars." Crystal said with the determination of a person who has nothing to lose.

"I can't give you the seventy five thousand. It's fifty thousand and that is written in stone but I will give you the ninety nine year free lease. If you get off your drunken high horse Crystal and start adding numbers you'll see that you come out ahead since the rent is free the $50,000 cash is pure gravy." Suki said with the authority of a decision maker.

"What's the catch?" Crystal asked Di Di.

"That is a good question. It's one of Mrs. Toyota's rendezvous apartments. She is shameless, she cheats front of Mr. Toyota's nose. He is going to screw her

by leasing the apartment to an American girl. Mr. Toyota figures that you are so totally self-centered that you won't be bothered crushing your best friend's mother's love life." Di Di said sober as judge, even though she finished a bottle of whiskey.

"Who the hell is my best friend?" Crystal asked puzzled.

"You have to consider the whole sentence Crystal. Who is Mrs. Toyota's daughter?"

"Why it's you Suki. Give me a hug my new best friend." Crystal said hugging Suki.

Di Di looked at the two young women with calculating eyes. Her battle with Mrs. Toyota is going to become interesting. She judged Crystal tenacious as bulldog, a good match for Suki's birth mother, Lila Toyota.

"Are you interested in the apartment?"

"Yes! I get a ninety nine year lease plus $50,000 and my apartment is returned in the same shape as it was before the work started."

Suki filled in the contract. Crystal skimmed the document and said.

"Please add that tenant or occupant must vacate premises when demanded by lease holder."

Suki rose to protest but Crystal made it clear that there was no compromise, "I am writing it in stone. If I don't get that sentence, there is no deal."

"That is the deal. Suki and I are the best of friends. Di Di, the Witch, and I get along barely."

Crystal nudged me and asked.

"You are not falling asleep are you Joseph?"

"I opened my eyes and I was back in the limousine heading for the airport. What happened to the apartment in Japan?" I asked.

"When I go to Tokyo it's empty but there are signs of occupation. I think Di Di the Witch informs Lila of my coming. For two years I got nowhere evicting her. The case was postponed and postponed and even the postponement was postponed. This went on until I went to Tokyo unannounced and walked into one Lila's cocktail parties, a totally decadent affair.

"There was a woman with a German Shepherd dog, the dog was her lover. The dog lover and a guy who must have been a hundred years old were discussing the pros and cons of loving donkeys and dogs. I sat in the corner watching the show and liking it. The old man broke away and came over to me." Crystal said dreamily.

"I think you will want to whip me when you find out that I am the person who is holding up your eviction petition in court."

85

"Whip you? I want to kiss you! I've never been to a party like this; everybody is a total degenerate."

"I think you should whip me anyway, because I will not let any American own this apartment."

'What makes you so powerful? I asked him surprised.

"I am a Japanese aristocrat, not much money, but lots of pull." The old man said with pride.

"How about twenty thousand dollars for a positive result in court." I offered looking at him with wonder.

"That is a lot of money but I can't do it. I am the top dog in this crowd. I can't go against the welfare of my lets say sex slaves." The old man answered cackling.

"I know the script sir. My nanny left the book on my bed when I was twelve years old. The name of the book is the Collected Works of Marquise De Sade. According to that script I would have to beat you, bugger you, and do all sorts of filthy things to you, just to be part of this superior crowd sir; but I just noticed I've a plane to catch so I must go." I said and got up to leave.

"Wait. The old man grabbed my arm with strong spidery fingers. I'll do it for $20,000. There is a jade I been wanting for sometime. The eviction order will be handed to her in a month. Here is my card. Send me a Bank Check when you receive the verdict."

"He let go of my arm and walked over to the dog girl and patted her dog. I caught Lila Toyota looking at me with angry tears in her eyes. She must have realized what happened, I won. I gave her a wicked grin and left. Twenty thousand dollars wasn't much money to find out how the game was being played. And it was neat to have a Japanese Aristocrat in my purse."

"You didn't have to spend twenty thousand to get Mom out of the apartment, father would have done it for nothing. All you had to do is ask him Crystal."

"I know my darling Suki but I don't need that type of favor and I don't think he could have outmaneuvered the old Aristocrat. It was a pleasure to turn the Aristocrat against your Mom and Dad."

"What do you think of the old man Joseph?" Suki asked.

"He sounds kinky." I said.

I was amazed that Suki was taking it so matter-of-factly I asked her.

"What do you think of all this Suki?"

"Nothing! I was in my final year of residency at Colombia Presbyterian. I was also taking a six-hour session on tropical diseases with the Centers for Disease Control. The time I spent with Crystal was fun time, I love her and I simply didn't have the time and energy to play my parents and Crystal's stupid game. Every three months Crystal would go to Japan and come back empty handed.

I didn't think my parents are doing so badly. My mother's luck changed when Crystal came to Japan and bribed the Ancient Aristocrat. That is the name of the old man who double crossed Mom for Crystal. The Ancient Aristocrat is a very generous yet a dangerous man he can order those who rank below him to commit Hari Kari. And since he created the Society of the Demented Clown everyone in the society ranks below him. Di Di told me the Ancient caused a boy to commit Hari Kari just to see how the ceremony worked; from his degenerate point of view.

The event went off beautifully. The boy who killed himself ritually was madly in love with one of the Ancient's geishas. She ordered him at the Ancient's bidding to prove his eternal love for her by committing Hari Kari. To encourage him she took a powerful poison. The boy in his grief dressed in white showed a razor sharp knife into his stomach from just above his pubic hair and then pulled it up violently all the way to his esophagus. Everybody present agreed he died heroically.

The Ancient's Geisha recuperated very nicely; she drank the antidote after the boy died.

The society bought the Geisha a gold locket with a photo of the boy's final seconds on this earth. The Ancient Aristocrat is high up in Japanese Society but there are those who are closer to the Palace. They were not pleased hear about the spectacle. They did not move against the Ancient, because it was a lover's tragedy but the Ancient was put on notice, no more.

There is another story about the Ancient that my mother told me on my twenty first birthday. The Ancient Aristocrat couldn't get an erection for two years. He tried Ginseng, deer antlers, oysters and all sort of exotic things nothing worked. An old Korean herb doctor told him that the Chinese eunuchs used to eat the brains of freshly killed convicts to get an erection. The Korean herb doctor thought, the whole idea was funny, but the Ancient took it seriously.

He mulled over the information for a year and decided the best bet was to get an accident victim's brain. He bribed a number of ambulance drivers. One of them delivered a severed head. The Ancient decided to make it a big ceremony of the meal he, invited the inner circle, of the Society of the

Demented Clown. There was a table with one chair in the center of the room. The Ancient sat in the chair. Everyone else stood in a circle around him. The company was dressed in the finest European clothes except for the Ancient who was dressed in his family's military regalia.

Someone brought in a cooler with the head of a twenty year old young man on ice. He died in a motorcycle accident. A surgeon who was a member of the society placed the head on a fine fifteenth century jade platter and proceeded to saw off the top of the skull. He removed the brain and placed it on a gold plate and stepped back. The Ancient was about to cut into the brain when the doors burst open.

Six men and a woman ran in to the room. The men were dressed in ancient samurai uniforms with swords. They also had M16 machine guns. Two women in charcoal black Kimonos entered the hall. One of the women carried white Hari-Kari clothes; the other one carried a pillow with the ceremonial knife resting on it. The third woman who ran in with the troop held a large sword and a rug. The commander of the Samurai troop leveled his rifle at the Ancients and said.

"We will form a circle around you so you can change to the Hari Kari clothes." Pointing to the women who carried the pillow he said. "There is the Hari Kari knife, there is the rug to kneel on, and the sword is to decapitate you after you committed Hari Kari, to end the pain quickly. Please honor one of us to do it, we are all from famous families, so you won't be dishonored. I recommend Hiro he is strong as a bull."

"Its not strength that counts but accuracy I will have the woman with the rug and the sword to do it." The Ancient said with a defiant bearing.

"We knew you would." the troop commander said with a studied smirk. He lowered his gun and so did the rest of the troop. The commander beckoned to the woman with the Hari Kari knife and in a guttural voice he said to the Ancient.

"We are ordered to let you eat the brain and then if it works you can have sex with anyone but my men and women. Once the fornication is over your grand finale will be to commit Hari Kari, got it?"

He let off a burst of the M16 rifle. The Ancient Aristocrat winced; rubbed his ears and said.

"I won't eat the brain right now and I won't commit Hari Kari. You have to bring me a note from the Power of Heaven before I commit suicide."

He burst through of the circle of Samurai and calmly walked toward the door. One of the women in black ran after him and produced a simple double typed page made of silk. The Ancient read it and turned ashen, it was an order to exterminate him and the whole society if he would have made the decision to eat the brain. She told him.

"This is the second time you have been noticed by Heaven. The Geisha's boy's Hari Kari was the first; that had certain romanticism but this is pure idiocy. You have used up all the merit gained while you worked for the government during World War II. This is the last warning from Heaven. The next time you pull a stunt that reflects on us it is going to be the knife or the bullet."

The ancient pissed in his uniform as he watched the troop leave taking the cooler, with the head in it, with them. Despite his fear he noted to the noble woman how sensual the piss felt as it ran down his leg. The woman looked down at the pool of urine collecting at the Ancients feet. She simply said.

"I am glad you understand the gravity of the situation."

She turned and followed the rest of the Samurai and Ladies out of the hall. The Ancient went back to the table and sat down. The society formed a circle around him and gave him a round of applause for a wonderful performance.

My mother like every other member of the society heard the woman give the Ancient the warning and she was scared for her life yet she decided to swear fidelity to the Ancient Aristocrat and the Society of the Demented Clown forever. She laughed and clapped with the rest of the crowd as the old man drank a water glass full of rice wine.

"Why are you idiot's laughing and clapping?" The Ancient asked. "I almost died."

"We are glad you decided not to go down with the ship." My mother said. "We would have drowned with you."

The Ancient took another swig of the rice wine and said. "Damn right." The company started clapping again but with a lot more humor."

"I met the ancient Aristocrat once at my seventeenth birthday party." Suki said wistfully.

"He showed me a picture of a man with a large penis. Pointing to the penis he said."

"This is what women live for. Keep it happy and you can reach the top in our type of world." He kissed my forehead and wished me happy birthday then he whispered in my ears.

"Welcome to your New World Suki that is like a Japanese Bonsai. The Bonsai tree to achieve its beauty is tortured by wires and clippers. That is life in a nutshell you can accept it or not it doesn't matter, it just happens."

Then without speaking to anyone else he left the party. Di Di had a fit when I told her what happened. She threatened to kill my mother if the old man ever came near me again.

Di Di not only has an Irish accent but she also has Irish morals. Despite what Di Di said I understood what the old man meant; I liked the thought's he set off in me when I played with myself that night."

"That's a pretty metaphor. Few more words like that and he could have screwed you on the front lawn no wonder Di Di was pissed." Crystal said with a yawn.

"The thing about the Bonsai Tree and life is true I don't care how cynical you are Crystal. What do you think Joseph?"

"I got what he meant; it is very beautiful and sad." I threw Suki a kiss and asked.

"Why didn't he just take Viagra? It is supposed to work for old man too."

"Don't be silly the brain thing happened a long time ago in the seventies. Now mom gets Viagra for him for free and he pops them like candy." Suki said tittering under her breath.

The limousine came to a stop front of the cargo terminals gate. There were a couple of Army guys with rifles guarding the entrance looking bored. We went through the metal detector with no trouble. A golf cart like contraption carried us to Suki's plane.

Suki explained that the sitting accommodation were tight because the plane was equipped to carry biological matter. I didn't think it was all that bad. There were two seats facing each other on each side of the isle. There was plenty of legroom. Crystal and Suki sat in chairs on one side of the isle while I faced an empty chair on the other side. The rest of the plane was equipped with stainless steel refrigerators incubators and many other exotic medical storage cabinets.

The pilot introduced himself to Suki and bowed a couple of times. Suki was gracious and shy. The ideal Japanese woman you see in the movies. Crystal instead of returning his bow stuck out her hand and shook hands with him. He seemed taken aback but pleased to shake hands.

When he bowed to me I had the urge to return the bow and I did then we shook hands. He told us we would be taking off in fifteen minutes and went back to the cockpit. Suki said that there were drinks and sandwiches in the refrigerator next to the bathroom.

I went and got a tuna sandwich and a diet coke; I was ready to fly. I closed my eyes after I ate and woke up as we were landing in Atlanta. I thought there was some kind of trouble with the plane but it turned out they were picking up and dropping off stuff for the CDC then we were flying to Miami, Florida.

I couldn't fall asleep. Crystal was in deep sleep her eyeballs were moving under her eyelids. Suki was reading a magazine.

"What are you reading?" I asked her.

"You are you awake Joseph? Thank God, I am bored to death."

She leaned over to me and whispered.

"I would make us both happy but everything on this plane is video taped. The tape would get back to my father. I hate for him to think that I enjoy sex. My mother's sex life is a big enough of a burden for him.

"What would happen if he found out?"

"That is a pretty stupid question Joseph. Don't you have parents?"

"Yes! I have parents Suki. My mother's emotional specialty is the guilt trip. Her bad trip started with the twenty-five hours of hard labor she went trough to have me. My father just took things away from me the car keys, the car, the allowance and my Fender guitar. He never spoke a harsh word but something was taken away from me for a while generally for two weeks. I forgot his punishments but Mother's guilt trips are still with me today. Do you think I should be held responsible for taking twenty-five hours to come out? They moved to Arizona five years ago. They only come to New York once a year, thank God."

"That's funny Joseph my father gave me things when I screwed up he didn't want me to feel bad. I love to please him. I became a doctor specializing tropical diseases, because he wants to expand the Company's presence in the tropics." Suki laughed.

"You need a degree in business administration for expanding a company don't you?" I asked.

"A pharmaceutical company lives and dies by research and development. I will head our tropical R&D.

"What do you really want to do Suki?" I asked.

"She wants to fuck." Crystal whispered rubbing her eyes.

Suki laughed bobbing her head up and down in agreement.

"How long have you been awake?" I asked Crystal.

"Long enough to know it's time for confessions." Crystal said yawning.

"Tell him about the Witch. How she got in to your life and why a Japanese woman has such a thick Irish accent."

"Di Di's father Miko Sugaro was a spy master. He was sent to Ireland from Japan to set up a spy network in England during World War Two. He worked out of the Japanese Embassy in Ireland. Ireland was neutral in the Second World War. His interest was political gossip that he also passed to the Nazi's. There were a lot of Irish domestics who worked for very important people in Britain; most had relatives in Ireland.

Sugaro, her father, built his network before the Japanese bombed Pearl Harbor. People who if approached by a German would turn the German in, would talk to him without suspicion. All they talked about was kitchen gossip. Sugaro was a master at pulling together from twenty or thirty different sources a trend in the British political elite's thinking.

His network gave the Germans and the Japanese a good idea how the British and the Americans would wage the war. It cost the Japanese government a lot of money to run his network of which seventy five percent ended up in Sugaro's pocket.

He had a large list of phony agents who received large sums of money for the intelligence that the domestic's provided for a free beer in the pub. The German's were grateful. The intelligence was so good that the Japanese Home Office paid Sugaro the money even though they considered him corrupt. No questions were asked.

Miko Sugaro was a cold man. He spent just enough money on the domestics to snare the workers, after the workers were compromised, they got nothing or bare minimum to cover genuine expanses. His favorite game was blackmail. His web had no elasticity to it; either you co-operated or you got tripped up."

Crystal interrupted Suki.

"What do you think he did with the money Joseph?"

"He put it in a Swiss Bank account that's a no brainer." I said.

"No" Suki said "I'll tell you in a minute how he invested two million pounds under the noses of the Japanese militarist's counter intelligence service. Sugaro was very shrewd man. When the Germans lost North Africa he saw the writing on the wall. He got in touch with his counterpart in British Intelligence and told him that he would feed any bullshit they wanted to the Nazis. He showed the British intelligence guys some of the work he was sending to the Germans.

It took the British ten minutes to buy into the scheme. Sugaro's work was so solid for so long that the Germans trusted his information implicitly no matter how outlandish it was. Now he was collecting from the Germans the British and seventy five percent of the working budget from Japan.

There is not much you could do with money if you are in the spy business. Sooner or later counter intelligence trips you up on a money transaction. But if you have a hobby that you had for years and everybody knows you have that hobby then you can get away with making two million pounds on the sly. He was a stamp collector. Certain stamp are so rare that there is always a market for them peace or war time."

I interrupted Suki.

"Two million pound buys a room full of stamps. Wouldn't somebody notice?"

"It doesn't take that many stamps Joseph." Suki said. "Sugaro bought five albums of stamps for two million pounds from a French family heading for Lisbon. There was a man at the United States Embassy in Lisbon who guaranteed them visas for a million dollars. They had to sell their hundred-year old stamp collection. Sugaro tried to get a bargain but they would not budge on the price. Sugaro was considering turning the family over to the Nazis and demanding the albums as a reward but he was afraid the Germans would steal the albums even from him."

I said.

"Shit! That's cold."

"Sugaro is cold and mean." Suki said. After the war Sugaro settled in Ireland. He ordered a bride from Japan. His mother selected the girl. His mother didn't even bother to send a photograph of his wife to be. The girl arrived on the plane and two days later they were married.

At this time after the war he worked for the Japanese Embassy in London but his power base was in Dublin. The British vouched for him and the American's allowed him to work in the Japanese Embassy as sort of a trusted caretaker. He had to report on his fellow workers.

His American Boss, Max Murphy, didn't like Japanese. He watched Sugaro like a hawk. Murphy was a trained Army Counter Intelligence Officer who spoke fluent Japanese; he was also a Certified Accountant just the type of guy to watch a spy handler like Sugaro. He heard from the British that Sugaro made quite a bit of money during the war. He decided he was going to get some of that money. He observed Sugaro's wire transaction. To Murphy's dismay every thing was up and up, Murphy built a war crimes case against Sugaro. He had no intention of arresting Sugaro, the British would have had a shit-fit, but it was good blackmail material.

The British told Murphy, after much hewing and hawing, the amount of money they paid Sugaro during the war and how much of his Nazi money they exchanged for British pounds but they swore up and down that they had no idea where the money went. The British said with total innocents that Sugaro spent the money on his spy network.

Murphy sized up Sugaro as a thief the first time he laid eyes on him. The way Murphy saw it there was no way that rat spent all that money on his net. Murphy, after great difficulty, managed to get, the Imperial Japanese Counter Intelligence files, on the Japanese Embassy in Ireland. Whoever wrote the files came to the conclusion that Sugaro was stealing money by the bucketful. However, they didn't touch him because his spy network was fantastic.

The author of the report also realized something that Sugaro never did that the spy network was not worth a dime without Sugaro's incredible ability to pull facts together and paint a clear picture. Their Nazi German allies were enchanted by Sugaro's work. Murphy also learned from the Imperial files that Sugaro lost large sums of money in Mote Carlo while visiting his fascist colleagues in Vichy, France. The Japanese counter intelligence source was a German officer who was slighted by Sugaro.

Murphy was stunned. Sugaro the son-of-bitch thief was a gambler. Murphy pulled in his horns and stopped his game, why waste time if there was no money in it. Besides that he was getting a lot of heat from the British to stop the investigation. Sugaro was their man Sugaro made special effort to be friendly with Murphy. To Murphy the brown nosing meant that the British tipped Sugaro off and Sugaro was trying to cover his ass.

At odd moments he wondered why Sugaro stopped gambling usually it's a hard habit to shake but before he could investigate further Murphy was transferred to Japan where he had lot bigger fish to fry."

I interrupted Suki again.

"So the stamp story is bullshit. Sugaro gambled the money away in Monte Carlo."

"It's the other way around." Suki replied. "He paid a Nazi German officer to report him as a heavy gambler to Japanese Intelligence in Tokyo. Heavy gambling losses were a way he could account for the money he had stolen. As long as he had no money, he was safe from Japanese Counter Intelligence sharks, who like Murphy would let you slide for the lion's share of the stolen money." Suki said triumphantly.

"How do you know both sides of the story? I can understand knowing about the Sugaro's side of the story. Sugaro told his daughter and she told you but where did you get Murphy's story?" I asked Suki.

"My father had Di Di investigated by an American firm, through them Murphy's report came up. We knew about Murphy's report before we knew about the stamps. Sugaro's life didn't stop at the end of the war." Suki said. "He married a simple Japanese peasant girl not too sophisticated in the ways of the world. She knew one thing though that a husband could hit his wife but he could not to knock her unconscious, because the soup was too hot. She made up her mind that she would leave him but not before she gave birth to a daughter; Di Di who was born in 1947. After Di Di's birth Sugaro's wife seduced a six foot three Irish man who only hit when he was drunk but that was no problem for her, because she could hide until he fell to asleep. They eloped to Australia.

Sugaro was thunder struck. He was sick for a week. As the weeks went on he stopped feeling sorry for himself and realized he enjoyed being alone. He didn't have copulate with his wife that he found distasteful. His mother flew in from Japan to take care of the baby and keep house for him. He fantasized that the baby was really the Irishman's but he could not deny the birthmarks that were in his family for hundreds of years.

Little Di Di was a spitting image of Sugaro's mother but the thought hunted him like a stone in a shoe. When Di Di turned six she went to a local school run by nuns. Di Di spoke fluent Japanese but her Japanese accent changed. Sugaro hated the accent. He beat her until she was black and blue but the child couldn't change her accent. After a while he realized there was nothing he could do about it so he pulled out of her life and let his mother take care of her totally.

When Di Di was seventeen she fell in love with an Irish classmate. Sugaro went insane. He tried to stab her with a kitchen knife but Sugaro's mother hit him on the head with an iron skillet. He was hospitalized with a heavy concussion it was touch and go whether he would live or not.

Di Di seeing him close to death felt sorry for him so she promised her dying father she would never go with anyone but a Japanese man. To her sorrow he recovered and she was stuck with a promise she had no intention of keeping.

Di Di was a bright student. She went Cambridge on the Japanese Governments expense. She became a professional student. She had relationships but mostly with women. When she turned thirty one she

I started wondering if Crystal being a virgin wasn't just a joke. Maybe she was a virgin. Highly unusual for the crowd she was running with and at her age, she must be in her thirties.

I told her.

"I won't do anything you don't want Crystal," swishing my wrist. Suki cracked up but steel came into Crystal's voice.

"You can't be one of those lovely men Joseph. I am never wrong about that type of thing."

"Relax Crystal. Your animal instincts are correct but right now all I want to do is to get off this plane and jump into a bed and sleep. A thousand years must have passed since I met you in the Club."

I am saying," Crystal said, "you better be oriented toward this." She pulled up her skirt and pulled her panties to the side.

The heat was up between us again. Suki covered Crystal's legs with a magazine she was reading.

"Sorry Crystal, but you will have to stay a virgin, a little longer. We can't do this type of thing on my father's plane. I don't want to embarrass him front of his employees."

"Good girl Suki Toyota." Crystal said almost weeping. "Why did you sex him up in your dad's apartment? Di Di was there, she is an employee."

"You are just jealous, Crystal." Suki said pulling down Crystal's skirt.

"No! I am not. You can have him a thousand times but I must have these moments of unbearable desire." Crystal said her nails digging in to the palm of her hand.

"I like both sex and desire." I said putting in my two cents. The two of women were talking as if I wasn't there.

"We know, Joseph but you are a man." They managed to say it in unison.

"Crystal the virgin thinks sexual desire is the ultimate feeling; so there is no reason to come down from that plateau. I think it's worth having sex for its own sake even if there is no desire but when there is desire it's just the icing on the cake." Suki revealed.

"Are you telling me, because she is turned on by me she won't give it up?" I asked.

"Yes." Suki said with a smirk.

"No. Things are different between us. I saved your life when Brown tried to kill you. As the Chinese say 'if you save someone's life they belong to you.' You belong to me Joseph, and if the only way I can imprison you is between my legs Joseph then that's how it will be." Crystal said earnestly.

"I am looking forward to it Crystal but remember we are not in China. For arguments sake what will buy my freedom?" I asked.

"A four carat diamond engagement ring will do nicely." Crystal replied.

"I will be jumping from the frying pan into the fire." I said.

"Yes." She leaned over to kiss me but the magazine that Suki was reading came between us.

"Not in my father's plane my beautiful friends."

"We are going to land in five minutes. Please put on your seat belts." The captain announced through the loud speaker.

I settled back in the seat gripping the arm rests. Suddenly a loud thud shook the plane. The wings went side to side. Crystal and Suki started screaming and I almost passed out from fear. The disturbance stopped fast as it came and the plane landed wobbly. We waited for a word from the pilot but not a sound came from the loud speaker. Suki and Crystal were silent. I told them I was going to the cockpit.

"I am coming with you," Suki insisted. Crystal was silent. She was somewhere else.

We opened the cockpit door and found the cockpit a mess. There was blood everywhere. The pilot was sitting in his seat unconscious. The front window had a large hole in it. The remains of a large bird was on the floor next to the pilot. It had long legs maybe it was a Heron. I turned the pilot's face toward me and to my shock I saw the birds beak stuck in the pilot's eye. I heard sirens at a distance but I did not pay attention to them.

I just stood there mesmerized doing nothing but Suki was working on the pilot's face trying to stop the blood pouring from his wounds.

A woman in an emergency services uniform led me back to the main cabin. She told me we were going to the hospital emergency room but we would have to wait until the pilot was removed from the cockpit. I didn't want to go hospital but Suki and Crystal didn't object so I went along with their decision. I don't know why but I was really angry. I wanted to punch the wall. I just managed to control myself. The emergency services people hoisted the pilot out of the plane on a stretcher. To my relief he was alive. Suki had blood on her dress and hands she must have saved him, because when she got to him arterial blood was pumping from one his wounds. Now it stopped. She was sobbing. She said the pilot apologized to her.

"He landed the plane with that horrible wound and he apologizes to me. He apologized to me. All this is too much. I just want to lie down and sleep. I have never been so scared in my life Joseph."

She looked around the cabin and said. "I got to do something about Crystal. She must be in shock."

Crystal whispered.

"I am in shock but I am not moving around, because I might have defecated. My legs and arms are numb and tingling."

"Don't worry about soiling yourself. We have disposable scrubs on board. I'll get you some. If you have to you can wash and change in the lavatory. You feel numb and tingly, because you have been tense and stiff since the accident. Why don't you let go of the armrest for starters?" Suki asked with a soothing voice.

Crystal shook her head. Suki gently pried Crystal's finger off the armrest and as if by magic Crystal let go of the other armrest and she regained total mobility. She kissed Suki on the forehead. Suki got her the scrubs just in case she needed it. Crystal went into the lavatory happy as a child. Meanwhile there was pandemonium around us. I asked Suki.

"Are the transplant materials a loss?"

"No they are not." Suki said. "There is a door under the hull that leads to where transplants are stored.

The ghouls got them before the pilot was taken care of. The rest of the stuff is probably shaken but salvageable. I am sorry I couldn't do anything for the pilot, the pain he suffered must have been incredible. We have morphine on board but it's not a good idea with head injuries. If he is lucky he only lost an eye but if the birds beak penetrated the bone and hit the brain then he will have problems."

A small fat man interrupted us.

"Are you passengers on the plane?"

I said. "Yes," suspiciously.

"I am here to represent you. I am Jack Douglas of Douglas A. Douglas."

A lawyer, my anger returned. I took a step towards him but Suki stepped in between us and said.

"We do need representation and I like an aggressive approach Mr. Douglas." She went back to her seat to get her pocket book. She withdrew a business card and wrote instructions on it. Handing him the card she said.

"My lawyers and I want aggressive representation. That fucking bird should not have been on the runway."

"If aggressive you want Ms. aggressive you get. What about you sir? I was ready to say I would go along with Suki but Crystal who came out of the lavatory without the scrubs grabbed my arm and said.

"We will take your card and check with our lawyers to see if there is a conflict of interest, Suki owns the plane."

"No, I don't. We lease the plane from Iho Forklift Company of Japan. They take care of everything including insurance. The only thing we pay for is the fuel." Suki said with passion.

Douglas didn't see it, because Crystal was standing behind him but Suki and I saw Crystal's jaw drop to the floor for a second. She composed herself but not before Suki shouted in triumph.

"I got you Crystal."

Douglas was bewildered but pushed on.

"I dealt with Iho Leasing before but I never heard Iho Forklift Co. Iho Leasing likes to drag the case out before they settle. Generally, it takes two to three years before they cough up the cash. But they do pay." Douglas chirped happily.

I got sick of Douglas and his callous act. I told him to get the hell of the plane before I sue him for aggravating my condition. My left arm and neck was still numb from the shock of the landing.

Douglas left the plane without taking offence. He also scattered dozens of business cards on the seats. He shook hands with the security guard and was gone. Money must have changed hands because the guard had a big smile on his face.

The whole conversation with Douglas must have taken five minutes but to me it seemed like an hour. The guy was a real creep. I couldn't understand why Suki hired him. Being first on scene didn't make the man a good lawyer in the courtroom.

The pilot was finally removed. The triage team came for us. Suki and Crystal refused to go to the hospital. I was debating whether I should go to the emergency room. My arm was still tingling. Like the women I did not to go.

I had no real choice in the matter because Di Di had my three million dollars. Without Suki Di Di would never find me. It was not that easy to say no to the emergency personnel. The doctors put up a real fuss. They wanted us to go to the hospital for observation. We had to sign

"Your father bought shares of nothing. Looking back it is very odd how I met your father. Who the hell puts a pool in a New York apartment and never uses it. He did it just too get close to me, probably for Sikura Iho. Suki what the hell is your Dad up to?" Crystal asked crying from annoyance.

"Don't get paranoid, Crystal. Looking back it may look like a conspiracy but it was random events that got us together. My father would never get into criminal activity. He would never allow himself to be the hatchet man."

"During the war my grandfather Toyota wanted manufacture heroin for the Chinese market but he was afraid of selling it directly to the Chinese despite the fact that the Imperial Government looked the other way."

"He wanted to but didn't do it, because prudence got better of him. By luck he met a Japanese guy and his wife from America at a convention for people in the legal pharmaceutical business."

"The guys name was Harrison Mota Lincoln and his wife name was Jasmine. He was my grandfather on my Mother's side. The Harrison's are full blooded Japanese whose ancestors went to America with Commodore Parry's Fleet after the Commodore opened the doors of Japan for the United States. Their Japanese family name was Mota before they changed it to Lincoln.

"When the founder, old man Mota arrived, he fell in love with America. The vast spaces made him free. He felt he could expand his wings, forever. He was also a first class herb doctor. He plied his trade from a wagon up and down the cost of California. His doctoring impressed a wealthy man so much that the patron opened a pharmacy for him in a little town near Los Angeles, because he wanted Mota to be near him. He changed his name from Mota to Lincoln. By nineteen forty one that little herb shop turned into a regular twenty store drug chain they also owned the little herb shop."

"My Grand Father Harrison Lincoln was a licensed pharmacist and the inheritor of the drug chain. He made a point of visiting Japan for three months in the fall and early winter to buy freshly harvested herbs directly from the farmers."

"When the war broke out in December Harrison and his wife were stuck in, Japan. Harrison and Jasmine, my grandmother and grandfather, had heroin habits. He brought enough heroin to last for four months but he had plenty of cash, his legitimate herb farmer's only accepted cash, so he had enough money for an additional four months but after that he had to look for a supply of money to buy heroin and pay for the house they were renting.

"Grand Pa Toyota and Harrison hit it off when they met at a pharmacist' convention. They discovered that their companies did business together before the war started. Grand Pa Toyota was one of those Japanese who did not think Japan was necessarily destined to win the war with the United States. Very few people in the business agreed with him. A good friend told Grand Pa Toyota to watch his Ps and Qs, because the thought control police were asking questions about him."

"He shut his mouth and started paying close attention to his business. The Chinese heroin market was bug in his bonnet. But he was afraid to use the family business. He knew government's had a way of changing policy over night. If he wanted to get into the Chinese heroin market he had to have a front man. Harrison was perfect for the job. When Grand Pa Toyota proposed the deal to Grand Pa Mota Harrison, he received a shock. Harrison Mota Lincoln turned him down cold."

"Grand Pa Toyota didn't give up that easily. He bribed a maid to steal Mota Harrison's stash of heroin and cash. Grand Pa Toyota waited a couple of days then called on Harrison. He expected to see two people in supreme discomfort but he didn't count on Jasmine Mota Lincoln, who was a packrat, she hid little bits of heroin here and there for emergencies. He was so surprised not seeing them in pain and agony that his face fell. Grand Father Harrison didn't say anything but Jasmine pulled a gun from a thigh holster. She said.

"*What you have to say had better be good.*" *In English, Jasmine's Japanese was good but it sounded foreign to most Japanese and when she was mad she slipped, without thinking, into English. Toyota didn't understand what she said but he got the gist of it.*

He simply said, "I have something for you." Then put a large box on the table. Harrison opened the box, making sure he was out of his wife's line of fire aimed at Grand Pa Toyota. There was a vase size bottle full of white pills. When Harrison removed the cap strong vinegary odor permeated the room. Jasmine relaxed without lowering the gun and said.

"*This shit smells very fresh.*"

"*The company produced it this week. You can keep it whether we do business or not." Toyota replied gingerly.*

"*We will do business Toyota. Harrison is afraid of losing his pharmacist license in the United States, but since we are stuck in this shit hole we have to do something with our time.*" *Jasmine spit out the words angrily.*

"*Harrison don't worry Japan will win the war.*" *Grand Pa Toyota said without much conviction.*

"*Like a monkey's ass. Anyway, what are you proposing to my husband?*" *Jasmine asked nervously waving the gun.*

Harrison said in English looking around.

"*Jasmine stop talking. There might be microphones. We are foreign Japanese and this guy might report our anti-imperialist remarks.*"

Toyota understood one word, microphone, out of the conversation between Jasmine and Harrison. He butted in.

"*There are no microphones in the house. I checked on your political status with a politician friend of mine who knows about these things. You are of no interest to Political Police. They have you down as harmless rich Junkies. But I watch my mouth. You never know what a patriotic neighbor might do.*"

"*What do you want from us?*" *Jasmine asked again putting her gun in her thigh holster giving him a look at her bush. Jasmine never wore panties. Toyota turned red. She said.*

"*Don't look too hard Toyota that's Mota Harrison's now and always.*"

Toyota regained his composure as he watched Jasmine take the bottle, full of heroin pills, into the other room. She turned back and said.

"*You did say we could keep the pills whether we do business or not with you?*" *She left the room without waiting for his answer.*

"*Yes, it's yours to keep Jasmine and Harrison.*" *Toyota said slyly* "*You know Harrison you should not let a woman wear a gun.*"

"*Look Toyota my wife is the Women's Pistol Shooting Champion of California. She is also California champion of the mixed men and women category. She also killed a man who tried to break in to our house. At my word if you ever rob us again Jasmine will kill you. Now let me hear your proposition and I want back, ten times over, the money you robbed from us.*"

"*Harrison this is Japan not the wild American West you can't go around toting guns and shooting people.*"

"*Who robbed who Toyota?*"

"*I know, I know, Harrison but it looked like a good idea at the time. I want you to open a factory to manufacture morphine, paregoric and heroin.*"

"*That's a tall order Toyota since my funds and my four moth old daughter are in the United States.*"

"Don't be coy, Harrison Mota, you know I will provide all the capital to put you in business. You manufacture just enough morphine and paregoric to look good and I will provide the wholesalers who will buy it from you. I will supply the heroin. It will go through a number of warehouses to you."

"You will sell the heroin in China. It will be your company's job to arrange for the sale and shipping. I will give you a few contacts in China but you must expand your customer base there, I intend to sell a lot of heroin."

"I see you are hiding yourself very carefully but what prevents the government from arresting me?" Harrison Mota asked.

"The Government is looking the other way for now. For every junky Chinese there is one fewer fighter against the Imperial Japanese Army or so they think but looking at your wife with the gun I don't think they are right."

"Mota Harrison went to China and set up a distribution network through local Chinese pharmacies. My Grand Father Toyota manufactured the heroin and Harrison Mota sold it in China. It may seem like a direct line but there were cutouts through three or four banks."

"They had one additional meeting then they never saw each other ever again. Business was going good until one day Harrison Mota Lincoln overdosed himself on heroin and died."

"My grandfather Toyota stopped manufacturing heroin overnight. He gave up a million dollar business. He didn't give it up, because he had guilt feelings about Harrison Mota. He gave it up, because he would have been exposed. This fear of being caught doing the wrong thing came down to my father and from him to me."

"My father, as a reaction to my grandfather never does anything illegal so if he did business with Iho Forklift he must think it's legal. My Grandma Jasmine mourned the loss of, Harrison Mota, all her life. When the war was over she went back to the States. Nobody touched their Pharmacies because the Anglo President they hired was honest. She had a bundle of money in the bank. She kicked heroin by using morphine for a good while then she stopped using it altogether."

"My mother, Lila Mota Lincoln, was raised by finishing schools in Switzerland. When she turned eighteen she chose a Japanese College where she met my father Toyota. They did not know there was a family connection until he took her home to meet his parents. Grand Pa Toyota recognized her name."

"Looking with hindsight my mother could have said meeting in college was setup by my Grand Pa Toyota. It wasn't a setup for my mother and it's not a set up for you Crystal it was, kismet. He just picked your house to buy a condo, because the price was right." Suki said hugging Crystal.

"Are you telling me you are a descendent of the Japanese who came here with Commodore Parry? You must be some kind of royalty among the American Japanese." Crystal said with wonder.

"Yes, they were respected not only in Japanese circles but also in Anglo American society. My Great Grand Father used to brag, according to my Grand Mother, that he was invited to the inauguration of every President from Theodore Roosevelt to Franklin Delano Roosevelt. He and my Great Grand Mother died in a car crash returning from a function in Washington D.C."

"Their chauffeur drank himself silly in the White House kitchen while my Great Grand parents were getting drunk upstairs with Presidential party. Only good thing was that they died fast. The chauffeur drove through a barricade and fell in to the river."

"My Grand Father inherited everything in 1939. He was 21 years old. He inherited ten stores and a ton of money. Within a year he opened six more stores depression or not people needed medicine. Socially he was a dud, because he preferred getting stoned to chitchat."

"He did send big checks to all the organizations granting him titles. People gossiped but the big checks balanced the gossip. Heroin was an undercoat in his life but his life passion was opening new pharmacies. He would have had thirty stores in a couple years if he didn't get stuck in Japan. He made a mint in Japan, which he invested in fine Japanese and Chinese Art. Mota Harrison figured the Japanese would lose the war and the Yen would be worthless."

"He thought he may have to answer some questions to the American authorities so he made sure every piece of art was genuine and that it had a traceable history, nothing looted. He stored them in a bonded warehouse in Hiroshima. Everything was lost when the atom bomb hit. My grand Father Harrison Mota didn't mind, because he was dead, but my Grand Mother Jasmine still bitches about it. They had everything insured but the insurance company refused to pay on loses due to nuclear attack."

"Who inherited the drug stores in America?" Crystal asked sharply.

"My mother Lila Mota Lincoln now Mrs. Toyota did. It was held in trust for her until she turned eighteen."

"Why didn't your Grand Mother inherit the pharmacies?"

"Because, my Grand Mother's parents owned acres and acres of citrus fruit that today is a good part of Los Angeles."

"When they got out of the camps in nineteen forty five they found their groves full of dead wood but as luck would have it houses were being built all around their groves. When they went to the Japanese interment camp they signed their property over to a honest Jewish man who returned it, when the war was over, for a tiny fraction for what it was worth. To make a long story short the family made a fortune in real estate. They built rental housing for returning GIs. When that petered out they built office buildings."

"My Grand Mother's brother inherited every thing but he was gay and had no children and committed suicide so he left the bulk of his estate to Grandma Mota Lincoln. When grandmother dies I inherit from her. My Grand Mother figures that my Mother has enough money from Harrison Mota Lincoln's pharmacy fortune.

"My Mother is insanely jealous of me, when it comes to my inheritance, otherwise she is a sweet heart. Whenever the subject of my inheritance comes up she becomes livid and curses like a truck driver. My grandma Jasmine Mota Lincoln has genuine concerns about my mother. My grandmother thinks Lila may go crazy and give all her money to that crazy society and to that vicious old man. She says she won't leave a penny of her money to my mother."

"Would your mother give the pharmacies away my dearest?" Crystal meowed and hissed like a cat.

"She might give away the net profit but never the stores Crystal. They are her soul. They are the link to her ancestors who went on an adventure with Commodore Parry."

"Once a year, from Sagittarius to Aquarius, she takes her grand Christmas tour of her American pharmacies, there are thirty of them now and hands out bonuses to the managers and employees."

She won't ever give away her stores. But I am happy that Grandmother will leave everything to me. Now, all I get is an allowance from my father who is bugging me to go to work in Indonesia." Suki said sharply.

"If my mother dies and she won't do that before I die. I inherit the pharmacies and the street blocks they are situated on. When the big moment happens I will marry a Japanese man whose family immigrated to the United States before nineteen hundred and one."

"When I was eight my mother and I conspired to drive out the Toyota conformist gene from our line and replace it with the rugged non-conformist American Japanese pioneering stock. As time went on, her tours in America, became grander. She threw big parties for us children. I liked it until I figured out she was matchmaking and what made it worse she was openly telling one of the Japanese American boy's parents of our secret plan to drive out the Toyota conformist gene. I went to Grandma Jasmine to complain."

"Grandmother made a couple of calls to the boy's parents then she called me in to her parlor and told me a secret about my mother that everybody in the family knew, but me, that Mom was an emotional idiot but she liked her plan but with a different family. Grandma and I nurtured the secret for two years then she blew it in a moment of anger and told my mother about it. Mom wouldn't talk to me for months."

"I only get one seventh of my father's fortune the rest goes to his six brothers and sisters and nephews. What a drag I want to inherit it all. Lately he has been tying my inheritance to the opening of the, Toyota Tropical Research Center, in Indonesia. He wants me to find a new bacterium that he can name after himself." Suki laughed.

"What happened to your ten year old beau?" Crystal asked yawning.

"He is into Hip-Hop."

"We are not turning you Joseph and me into a foursome are we?" Crystal asked intensely bored.

"He is into junk. Grandma Jasmine reels him in and reels him out." Suki said looking at me.

"Is he one of your Grandma's pharmacists?" Crystal asked through a yawn.

"No, he is the salt of the earth. He couldn't make it trough pharmacy school. He manages a couple of Toyota warehouses in Los Angeles. Whenever he shows up at a party it is Grandma's way off reminding me that it's about time to get married."

"Is he the gene pool, that's going kick the Toyota gene pool, to independence?" Crystal asked yawning again.

"Brains are not everything. His family specialized in herbs for the Mota Lincoln Apothecary Shops during the turn of the Twentieth Century and now they sell herbs to New Age Stores. Japanese style of farming requires a lot of bending, strong legs, and patience. His got both. My grandmother Mota Lincoln pampers him. That is why she lets him have junk. Anytime he wants some she gives it to him. She is not judgmental even though she gave it up."

"However, my mother has a strong rule for the pharmacist she employs, if they sample the product they sell, they don't work for Mota Lincoln Pharmaceuticals. If security finds a licensed pharmacist sampling the product, they are let go with a large severance pay and paid counseling."

"Where does your grandma get her supply when she is in her heroin persona?" Crystal asked.

"Trust me now?" Suki asked.

"I trust you!" Crystal said.

They reached to shake but yanked their hands back at the same time and burst out laughing.

"She makes it from scratch. I don't know where she gets the opium but she told me she only made it for two people. She made it for herself and for her deceased husband Harrison Mota Lincoln and I now I guess, for my hip-hop husband to be."

"She took pity on him. She invites him to her house on his birthday to make up for my mother bad mouthing him as stupid kid. Two years ago she found out he was on junk, because he showed up stoned and an abscess size of a quarter in his arm. He looked like a wet puppy to Grandma Jasmine. She applied her womanly arts and cured the abscess with herbs and promised to give him heroin, whenever he asked for it."

"To me it looks like she is keeping him, nice and pickled, waiting for you to collect him, Suki." Crystal laughed.

"It maybe so," Suki said seriously.

"I have a pickled, Japanese American Hip-Hop man waiting for me, weird. What do you think of all this Joseph?"

"I don't go for foursomes unless it's paired off double dating. When are we arriving to your house Crystal?"

"You must feel threatened, Joseph by my Hip Hop Japanese boy?" Suki asked. She stretched her legs and her modest skirt rolled up giving me a good shot of her bush. The heat in me shot up.

"Yes, I feel threatened. I like this scene with you two. There is nothing like it." It sounded like bravado even to my ears but it was the truth. This seemed like awfully long ride to Miami.

"When are we arriving to your house, Crystal?" I asked again.

"Not for a while. I changed our destination to north of Miami. I don't know how long it will take but we will get there sooner or later. I will discuss Iho Forklift Co. with you later Suki."

"What is in Orlando besides, Disneyworld?" I queried pissed, because I was exhausted and wanted to sleep.

"The headquarters for the Zany Toy Foundation is in Orlando. That is my mother's sense of humor and it's a lot of fun for my employees. If Mr. Iho managed to buy any of my companies I will fire the whole Pacific desk. Suki you told us lot of stories of your family but I am not convinced that your father is on the up and up." Crystal said with the voice and the demeanor of an executive of a big corporation, who was being screwed.

"I told you about my grandmother, because she can be an ally against my father's family." Suki interrupted, "She hated my Grandfather Toyota because, he ripped off her stash of heroin. I guess you have to be a heroin addict to understand the hatred she nurtured for him. She also hated him, because she blamed him for the bad batch of heroin pills that killed her husband Harrison Mota Lincoln. She tested one of the pills and it was twice as strong as the normal pills they were selling and using.

"The minute Grandfather Toyota heard that Mota Harrison overdosed he sent the police to Grandma's house to confiscate her guns. Then shamelessly told her it was for her benefit, because he was afraid she would try to commit suicide. Grandma Jasmine also holds a grudge against my father for tricking my mother into marrying him. She like you doesn't believe that it was just a chance that they met at the University."

"See neither do I!" Crystal said biting her nails.

I kept my mouth shut. I had no idea where this was leading to.

"Look Crystal you have very strong allies in me and Grandma Mota Lincoln. She hates Dad's two brothers but she gets along with his four sisters and my uncle's wives. The only woman she doesn't get along is my father's mother. My Grandma Toyota is a battle-ax; she gave birth to seven children but she has no brains for business or anything else."

"She was a punching bag for, Grandpa Toyota so long, that for her it was the norm. Grandpa Toyota left his holdings evenly divided between his seven children with one proviso that they let my father run the business for ten years, then if they were not satisfied with the result they could replace him."

"My father was a good choice he built with help from one of his brothers an empire worth billions. His two brothers and four sisters enjoy the financial benefit, without doing anything."

"Some of my aunts wanted join the firm but the brother's wouldn't let them. The four women had the majority shares but they would have had to go to court to enforce it. That was unthinkable for Japanese women, at the time. Grandma Mota Lincoln tried to encourage the women to fight their brothers in court but the women were creatures in their society so they shied away from a fight."

"Even though Grandpa Toyota reached top levels of society he dealt with women like a street thug. He beat Grandma and the girls with punches sticks and belts. Half the time grandma sported black eyes. His geishas suffered the same treatment. He didn't like women."

"Couple of years ago one of my aunts named Butterfly told me she saw Grandmother Jasmine Mota Lincoln kill Grandpa Toyota. It was during a big party celebrating Grandma Toyota's Birthday. Grandma Toyota was wearing pancake makeup to hide the bruises on her face. Everyone was happy drinking wine and eating like elephants. Only Grandma Toyota sat there swaying."

"She didn't eat anything. She sat there as if she was lost on another plane. On-the-other-hand, Grandma Jasmine Mota Lincoln drank like a fish. She was challenging the men to a drinking contest. Grandpa Toyota who had quite a few accepted the challenge."

"His daughter's tried to stop him, because they were embarrassed by the whole scene. Grandpa Toyota and Grandma Mota Lincoln started drinking whiskey. He handed her a shot glass that she drank. She handed him a shot glass that he drank. The more Grandma Jasmine Mota Lincoln drank the stronger she seemed to get. Grand Pa was getting woozy drunk. According to Butterfly, Grandma Jasmine Mota Lincoln reached into the sleeve of her kimono real fast and put something into his shot of whiskey."

"Grandfather drank it and in a minute or two keeled over dead drunk. After a while he turned blue then he stopped breathing. No one noticed that he was dead, because most of the family followed Grandpa and drank themselves silly. Grandma Toyota was there but she was in her masochistic paradise."

"Butterfly stayed sober so she could watch over Grandmother Toyota. One of the maids discovered that the master of the house was dead as a doornail. He was taken directly to the funeral parlor. The boys missed the old man but the women felt cozy with his passing." At the funeral Grandma Toyota hissed at Grandma Mota Lincoln. "I hate you for taking my husband away, you American tramp."

"From that point on Grandma Jasmine Mota Lincoln stopped eating food or drinking at the Toyota residence."

"What's the point of all this Suki? Are you telling me that your Grandmother will kill your father to protect me?"

"Are you out of your mind Crystal? Do you think I would let anyone touch my father? It's family politics. There are more women in the Toyota house than men. Except for my Grandmother Toyota they all like Grandma Mota Lincoln's free American attitude."

"They are my mother's generation. They look up to Grandma Mota Lincoln. Grandma Mota still runs her own business. That gives her a lot of respect among the women. Are you getting the drift of what I am saying to you Crystal darling? The sisters own a lot of shares. Together they own more than my father and the uncles. They will listen to Grandma Mota Lincoln and they will jump all over father if he endangers the family business with criminal activity."

"She is wild but she is solid as a rock when it comes to business. She dumped her real estate holdings in Japan before the crash in the nineties. She advised the family to do the same. To everybody's surprise my father took her advice. He sold all the speculative stuff. He held on to the land under the factories. He made out like a bandit."

"How did you make out during the real estate speculation in Japan, Crystal?"

"Pretty good Iho Forklift and its subsidiaries are leasing companies. We lease ocean going vessels, oilrigs, farmland, high-rise buildings and motor vehicles. You name it we lease it. We have quite large land holdings in Japan. The value of the leases were going up but that didn't help me, because I leased properties at a fixed rate."

"I went to a Gypsy fortuneteller who told me not to worry. Real-estate speculation always ends with crashes but leases at a fixed rate retain their value."

"We made a few purchases but those were a steal. We couldn't pass them up."

"Otherwise, Iho Forklift stayed a quiet old fashioned company. I like it better that way. Sometimes I go down to the waterfront and watch an Iho leased containership being unloaded a warm feeling comes over me. I own that ship. I own one hundred percent of it."

"Remember that Suki Toyota. I own one hundred percent of Iho Forklift. Mr. Iho is just a figurehead. A well paid figurehead but a figurehead never the less. Mr. Iho gambles. There is an office at headquarters that keeps track of his betting. If his debts get too heavy we cut back the cash until he gets his act together. We slowly cover his loses then we let him lose again."

"I think he likes the anticipation of getting cash again as much as he likes playing poker. I don't pay much attention to him. I just read the reports of the Foundation Directors titled 'Keeping Iho happy that he sends to my Investment Bank in Zurich. Iho doesn't know I exist. My father was funny that way the fewer people who knew the family the better he liked it. Of course everybody in the ballooning crowd knew me but that was a different rabbit hole. My rabbit hole didn't have an outlet in Japan. Until you and your father popped in to my life Suki Toyota."

"If you ladies don't mind if I interrupt what will Di Di do with my three million dollars? Is it going to find me if we are being shanghaied to Orlando?"

"That's not my business." Crystal said coolly.

"Di Di will find me. She always does. You will get your three million, Joseph." Suki said patting my thigh.

"I don't like this situation at all." I said. I reached for the car lock but they were stuck in the down position.

The window partition rolled down slowly an around six foot ten inches tall blond man with a thick Swedish accent asked Crystal if it was alright to unlock door. Crystal shook her head and said. "No."

Suki started screaming "You bitch! Where is my Korean driver?"

"He is learning Swedish, my lady." The giant laughed as he rolled up the partition.

"Don't worry Suki. We are going to my mother's castle. There is this marvelous castle in Bavaria built by a mad King named Ludwig. My mother liked it so much she made copy of it, on a smaller scale of course but a very good copy. It has a working dungeon and that's where you are going Suki Toyota if you take a step out of the castle proper. A high wall surrounds the castle. You are confined to the castle and if you try to escape it's the dungeon until I figure out this Iho Forklift deal."

The speaker squawked.

"Mum it's a good idea to collect their cell phones." The Swede rolled down the partition and put his hand out. I gave him my phone, Suki balked. "No." Looking at Crystal defiantly she said. "You can't make me." The Swede reached back then grabbed Suki's calf and squeezed hard. Suki yelped and threw the cell phone at her tormentor which hit the Swede in the face. Without blinking he said. "Thank you miss." Then he rolled up the partition.

"It serves me right." I said to no one. "Who hands in his right mind hands over three million dollars to a stranger." I looked at the two women. Suki was the personification of anger. She was ripping the car seat with her high heel shoes.

"Why didn't you help me Joseph?"

"Because, he is driving at seventy miles an hour. If I started fighting with him we would have crashed and we would have died Suki."

"Bullshit! You are scared of him!" Suki stuttered with rage.

"Listen Suki, your father hooked up with a person who from what I gather is very dangerous to Crystal. I don't think Crystal thought it through but I think she is holding you hostage."

"Don't be so melodramatic Joseph. Suki is my friend and she has the run of the castle and grounds but no one goes outside until I get to the bottom of this Iho Forklift thing."

"What about the dungeon?" Suki asked.

"That's the place for you if you try to leave. The dungeon is not that bad it is a copy of fashion Barbie's bedroom."

What's the color scheme? Suki asked excited.

"Pink of course," Crystal said laughing.

"I have the biggest collection of Barbie dolls. I am sleeping in the dungeon tonight," Suki said anger gone. She threw a kiss at Crystal. Crystal threw the kiss back at her.

I decided that I would have to be careful choosing sides with these women.

The houses started thinning out. The grounds around the houses started getting bigger. The houses became grander.

Crystal said. "We will be there in a couple of minutes."

We arrived, to a huge estate, a tall wall's covered by a jungle of runners and flowers was around it. A huge wooden door was sliding open horizontally. The Swede drove us onto emerald green grounds.

Uniformed staff stood on the grass, in the middle of the sixteen men and women, stood a distinguished looking guy in a pinstriped suit. The rest of the people wore starched uniforms. The scene was straight out of the movies, we got out of the car and the Swede drove off. We walked up the tile covered pathway. The guy in the pinstriped suit met Crystal. She extended her hand which he took and kissed.

"Very nice to see you Mademoiselle, welcome home, Crystal."

"These are my friends Suki and Joseph. We are playing a game that nobody leaves the grounds until I say so. Joseph can leave but if he is smart he will stick to Suki, if he wants his money from Di Di."

Suki lifted her skirt slightly and said. "Stick it to me all night Joseph." Then she turned to Pinstripes.

"Would you like to kiss this?" Suki asked pointing to the bushy hair coming out of her bikini panties that she must have put on in the car while I wasn't looking.

Pinstripes a bit unsteadily said. "Whatever Mademoiselle Toyota desires."

"Whatever Mademoiselle Suki Toyota wants." Suki mocked him.

Suki dropped her skirt and extended her hand. Pinstripes kissed it.

"Extend your hand Joseph so he can kiss that too." Suki said sarcastically.

"Don't be crude Suki. William is the manager of the estate not a clown." Crystal growled as we walked over to the staff, standing rigidly, on the lawn. After an awkward moment I stuck my hand out that William shook firmly.

Crystal thanked the staff for the nice welcome. They thanked her for coming home then each person returned to their duty. The cook stayed. William ordered him to leave but the cook stayed. Finally the cook said.

"What will it be breakfast, lunch or supper mum? Looking at you closely I think hot chocolate and Kailua is the right medicine."

I said.

"That sounds great to me. Bring me a quart."

Crystal turned to Pinstripes and said.

"William please inform the cook that your job description includes you as my personal butler and chief medicine man. So if the cook has ideas for my well being, please pass them trough you." Turning to the cook she said. "Cook lets not forget the chain of command. If you have complaints against this, use the suggestion box. William I will take a quart of that chocolate grog the cook is paddling."

The cook laughed and said.

"I like a house that understands the chain of command. I'll make the grog extra strong for you miss."

William said.

"Cook! Why don't you have the pastry cook make the chocolate and I will provide chocolate liqueur from the wine cellar and you mix it together,"

"Since when does a butler tell the cook how to run his kitchen?"

"What hat are you wearing right now William?" Crystal asked firmly.

"The estate manager of course." Crystal gave him a withering look. William turned to the cook and said. "Make up the grog and I will serve it."

It was about time they stopped bickering, I had enough, I was dead tired. All I wanted was a bed. Splendor and luxury surrounded me but I couldn't appreciate a thing. A young maid led me to a room. I plopped on the bed and fell asleep without taking my clothes off.

I woke up with a start. There was an incredible pain in my crotch. I opened my eyes to see Crystal's face an inch from mine.

"I am sorry Joseph, but I had to wake you up. There is an emergency at the front gate."

"Crystal, honey baby, that's no way to wake me up." I said rubbing my crotch gingerly. I looked around. The room was magnificent. Columns in the corners supported a domed ceiling. Frescoes of a hunting scene in rich primary colors covered the dome and the walls. There was gold gilding everywhere. Crystal stood above me like nymph in a see through nightgown. Despite my pain I became aroused and grabbed her and wrestled her under me.

There was a loud knock on the door. Pinstripes walked in without waiting for an answer. He was carrying a shotgun. My libido dropped to the floor. Crystal gave me a kiss and got off the bed. She and Pinstripes went to the window. I joined them after pulling on my pants. They were freshly cleaned. I did not remember taking them off.

Pinstripes opened the window. The big door to the castle had a little door that was open. The door was flooded with a spotlight. The big Swede was lifting a small person in a long dress off the ground. The smaller person was struggling valiantly but the Swede knew his business and held tight despite fact that he was getting kicked quite often. Suddenly there was a shriek.

"I am FBI."

The Swede dropped the woman like a hot coal. She showed him something. He stopped blocking the way. The Swede and the woman walked up the path toward the castle. My heart froze. Crystal turned pale. She said as we were walking to meet the agent.

"Oh, God they found Brown's body."

"Don't be silly miss. Brown died of a heart attack in Harlem Hospital. He was cremated, as he wished. His ashes were thrown in the East River," Pinstripes said. "Nevertheless, I won't let that woman in the palace without a warrant."

Suki joined us. "What's the commotion?" she asked.

She was dressed in a lightly see through beige nightgown. The snake started stirring in my crotch. We reached the lawn before they reached the castle's entrance. I took one look at the woman berating the Swede and I started laughing so hard that my side hurt. Suki jumped around the woman and grabbed her hands and they danced around like children.

"Di Di! Oh, Milk Mother! I knew you would find me. I told you Crystal. Di Di would find me. To Di Di she said. "They threatened to put me in a dungeon. You don't know how much I suffered."

"Di Di I am going to put you both in the dungeon if you don't tell me how you found us." Crystal asked her face was dark with anger.

"Suki, you can stop lying, you slept in a guest room just like Joseph," Crystal whispered in a sarcastic tone.

"Are you angry with me Crystal? What about me? I was supposed to meet you guys at the Blue Mariner Hotel. I didn't find you guys there. They told me you didn't check in. I called the airport and they told me your plane made a hard landing and that there were casualties. I thought I would die. I went to the airport and talked to one of the muck-a-mucks. He told me only the pilot got hurt. I relaxed a little bit. But something was wrong, because not only Suki's but Joseph's cell phones were turned off. I don't know your number so calling you was a wash out Crystal."

"Frantic, I went to the airport lounge and had a whiskey sour to think. The place was a wreck. I asked bartender what in the hell happened? He said two limousine drivers got in to a fight. A giant Nordic looking guy and a pretty husky Korean got into a fight."

"The Korean guy made some fancy Karate moves but the giant dislocated his hip with a grab. The Korean fought leaning against the bar but the giant grabbed him and dislocated both his arms. I asked him if he knew the Korean driver's name. Yes, he got all the information before they took him to the hospital. His name is Robert Park and he was in Miami

General Hospital. He is Mr. Toyota's driver. He flew down to Miami to meet the plane."

"You wrecked Bobby? He is the nicest guy. He never starts a fight. He only finishes them. He is also a triple black belt champion," Suki said angrily.

"Well, he didn't finish this fight. He is not so nice miss." the Swede answered. "He is homophobic. I just told him he had lovely eyes with my wrist hanging limp. He couldn't resist beating up a faggot. After I got through with him he was in so much pain he didn't notice I lifted the limousine keys from his pocket. That was the point of the fight. My fighting style is Jujitsu, which has an answer for every move. That and thirty years of contact fighting beat him. I started when I was ten years old miss. I was a very clumsy boy so my dad enrolled me in a Jujitsu class." The Swede did a pirouette. "Now I am quite supple."

"But stupid I show him a credit card and yell FBI and he lets go. Next time you ask for a warrant stupid." Di Di said with venom in her voice.

"That was not a credit card Madam. That was an FBI identification card with Ministry of Justice written in Japanese on the bottom. I dropped you fast and let you in, because I have a green card. In six months I will be eligible to become citizen. I will not screw it up, for an old lady, a dangerous old lady. She had this gun in her sash and two bottles of something in her Kimono sleeve."

Di Di turned crimson and kicked him in the shin. "You bastard, I thought I had you."

The Swede bent down and whispered in her ear but it was loud enough for everyone to hear if you don't stop kicking me I will make love to you right here on the lawn."

Di Di started giggling. She started swaying like a snake. Her arms were up in the air. She said through giggles. "You wouldn't dare?" He smirked "Yes I would."

Suddenly she pulled herself together and said giggling. "Ten years ago I would have kicked your shin purple; now I'll just leave you alone. There is more to you than meets the eye big man." She grabbed at his crotch and held it for a second then she turned around and ran toward the castle giggling.

"That's disgusting." Suki said to, no one, out loud.

"I didn't think she had it in her. Swede you are a marvel but how did she get in?" Crystal asked the Swede.

"My name is Freddie; Mademoiselle. She crashed her car into the gate three times before Tweed sent me down to check it out. We may have to replace the gate door."

"I am sending the bill to you Suki." growled Crystal pissed "You can go Freddie. Next time grab them before they get in. Before you go Freddie how did she find us? The Korean didn't have our address."

"Yes my lady I will grab them as long it's not against the law. Besides, Tweed is security I only do what he tells me to do."

Before Freddie had a chance to say anything more Pinstripes answered.

"It must be a satellite anti-theft tracking device. Freddie go through the limo and disable it. We don't want any angry Korean's coming here."

The Swede said glumly.

"I should have looked closer. It's an old Lincoln limo. I didn't see any obvious security devices just a regular old alarm. It didn't turn on, because I had the keys. The Korean must have liked gadgets. The lady also had a piece of paper in the sash of her kimono. It says Magnitude Security Devices and an eight hundred number to turn on the device on and an eight hundred number to turn the device off. Man! This is going to bring the cops."

"Don't worry she won't call the cops. As long as Suki is all right she won't call the cops. Suki and I were in too many hassles in the last couple days for her to bring the heat. If the car she crashed against the gate is drivable then drive it through the back gate and put it in the stable. Don't be nosey. Don't touch anything except the navigation device. Remove it and give it to William. If her car won't start call a tow truck. But before you do that bring all the baggage from the car up to the house without looking at the content. I will call the eight hundred number to shut off the device." Crystal dictated with authority in her voice. Authority rested on her shoulders like a mantle. She was in her element giving orders.

"Yes, Madam. What you said put my mind at ease. I'll do as you say."

"William!" Crystal shouted pointing toward Di Di who was running toward the castle.

Pinstripes ran after Di Di. He managed to stop her before she could enter the castle door.

"Where is the warrant FBI agent?" He shouted at the same time locking the breech of the shotgun but pointing it pointedly away from her.

"You see that Japanese girl over there I was her wet nurse and now I am her maid. That is my warrant." She pushed through the door still giggling. She turned around and asked him "Who the hell are you? Show me Suki's room."

"William Tweed mum." Pinstripe said. "You are welcome to our servant's quarters they are quite elegant."

"Nice name. I'll come to the servant quarters after I look at Suki's room." Di Di giggled.

"I thought so when I chose the name. This is the way to Suki's guest room."

"I haven't had so much fun in ages." Di Di laughed.

"I can't say I did." Tweed said without humor.

We caught up with them. Suki grabbed my arm and hissed at Di Di.

"I am not talking to you any more Di Di. That was a disgusting performance, an old woman like you grabbing a man's crotch, front of everybody."

"Do you have Joseph's packages Di Di?" Crystal interrupted.

"Yes, your highness they are in the car."

"Suki stop whimpering. You must feel the way I felt when my parents made love in the guest bedroom, when they thought I was sleeping. Disgusting, but I stayed curious about the act," Crystal said in dreamy voice. "William what's happening to her car?"

"Freddie can't start the car. He will get the tow truck from the stable. Meanwhile, he is bringing up the suitcases. He said he found the gadget that goes with those phone numbers. He shut the system down. He said there are no bugs in her rental car."

Di Di reached into her sash but there was nothing there except her credit card and the FBI identification card.

"Why didn't he take my ID and the credit cards?"

William said.

"Because, dear lady, you had them in your hands when you came on the grounds. But he had a chance to read the FBI card. He is convinced that you are a police agent on exchange from Japan to the United States. You have full police powers."

Di Di turned to Suki. "You see the things I do for you my love. It took a lot of money and two years of schooling before they gave me that card." She reached for Suki, but Suki shrank back, and said.

"Not with that hand. I will need time to get used this situation." Suki stuttered then she ran to her room.

"When is that lummox going to bringing my bags?" Di Di asked impatiently.

"Freddie does not enter the living quarters. A maid will bring the luggage here or to your room in the employee's residence." William said in an even tone.

"Give her a guest room William. We don't want her snooping around the servant's quarters. Bring her luggage to Joseph's room." Crystal ordered with crisp voice.

Di Di looked around and said.

"Let me guess. This is styled after Mad Ludwig's Bavarian castle. I know it is on scale but it lacks the grandeur of the open spaces the original's ground has. It's like a plum to a prune."

"Thank you Ms. Sugaro. Since we are talking to each other can you tell me how Mr. Toyota chose to buy an apartment on Park Avenue and what is this about Iho Forklift Company?"

"I don't know much about the apartment's purchase. Lila Toyota said he wanted a fancy apartment in New York. He was tired of the corporation suites the company owned. His taste became grand after he met Mr. Iho of Iho Forklift. Who is a fabulously wealthy man. All he does is gamble. Every once in a while he goes to a Tokyo Buddhist Temple where he insults the monks. I thought he supports the temple but on the contrary he goes out every day to beg food from the restaurants around the temple dressed in a monk's clothing." Di Di said as she followed me to my room.

I was so zonked when we I arrived that I didn't notice that a guestroom meant a little apartment with a bathroom and a good sized living room. I was listening to their conversation with a half an ear, because I was waiting for Pinstripes to bring the bags.

The three of us sat in my living room. It was gorgeous like the rest of the castle. I was like a junky waiting for his shot impatient to the ninth degree. Finally I said.

"Where the hell is William?" Just as Pinstripes walked in carrying four bags he gave me a sour look and said.

"I only have six hands your worship."

I didn't have a fast come back so I didn't thank him. Crystal thanked him pointedly. Even Di Di threw me a dirty look, thanking him.

All I wanted was my money. After asking Pinstripes to leave, Di Di went through her baggage in slow motion. She had a change of clothing for Suki. She had a change of under clothing for herself. She had some extra red sneakers and a couple of Kimonos, which were exact duplicates of the one she was wearing. She was doing a baggage striptease. I was patient outwardly but inside I felt like strangling her. Suddenly with flourish she threw a small duffel bag at me, and said with a high pitched laugh.

"There is your money minus fifty thousand transportation fee."

"Transportation fee Di Di?"

"Yes, you worship an additional transportation fee. I notice you fit into this castle very well. You no longer thank people for doing something important for you."

"I looked in the bag and there they were three packages of hundred dollar bills. I turned to Di Di and said.

"Thank you Di Di but you have to admit fifty thousand is kind of steep."

"Considering the adventures I had to go through I should have taken a hundred thousand dollars Joseph."

"Of course you are right Di Di, but it has been hell all around. I didn't think we would survive the plane crash. I am surprised I didn't wet my pants. How is the pilot?

Di Di answered with wonder in her voice, "he is a cold man. He lost an eye but instead of bitching about it he was discussing how much money he will make with an eager beaver young lawyer."

"The lawyer told me that you three were alive but suffered from heavy emotional trauma.

I have his card somewhere. He wants you to get in touch with him." Di Di searched through her handbag.

"Don't bother looking for his card, he managed get on the plane before the ambulance crew did. He gave us a whole bunch of cards. I want him to represent me. Crystal doesn't want him. The guy is too pushy for her taste. And as usual Joseph can't make up his mind." Suki said, her eyes turned away from, Di Di.

Di Di's cell phone rang. Di Di answered then she listened, just saying an occasional "yes" for fifteen minutes. She disconnected the line and just sat there without a word. Suki hugged her then shook her hard.

"What the hell is wrong Di Di?"

"That was Peter Wong my private English detective. Cathy Chin is on the loose. She sold her Security Agency to the highest bidder. Young Wong the Men's Association's new Boss was a major bidder."

"Miss Chin also gave the new boss a gift of thirty thousand dollars in a red envelope. It wasn't much considering the millions she made selling the agency to the new Boss's group. But it showed respect to the new Boss. Before accepting the gift the new Boss told her no wars with anyone period."

"Cathy Chin humbly told him she had no intention to start a war, instead she would become a Buddhist nun. She will shave her head and receive training in New York for six weeks. Then, she will travel to California for further instructions about Buddhism. After three months there she will go to Taiwan for contemplation."

"Our Peter Wong was one of the bidders for Chin's Security Company. He didn't have to tell me that he was a bidder but he felt he owed it to me after years of profitable service. That's his way of telling me he is no longer loyal to me. I feel betrayed. Peter has ideas about becoming Sir Peter a Knight of the British Empire. We will see if I could throw a monkey wrench in his plans. Not now, maybe five years from now, so he won't associate me with his shattered dream."

"We have six weeks while she is studying in New York to get her. Or we have three months to get her in California. I doubt she will go to California though. Soon as she is out of sight of the new Boss she will hunt for us. I say lets go up to New York and shoot her before she has a chance to get us." Crystal hissed all excited.

"Hold everything. I am not shooting anybody. Freddie reminded me that there are sane ways of handling situations without breaking the law. Besides, she might be real about becoming a nun." I told Crystal.

"Fool," Suki said.

"Gullible," Crystal said.

"Joseph, she must of had a fire sale the way these guys were falling all over themselves to buy Chin's business. I gather she got millions for the business, because there were groups of men bidding and they had to pool their money. It's quite possible that she is serious about becoming a nun but I doubt it. We should hire a private detective agency and have her followed twenty-four hours a day. See where she goes from New York." Di Di said through a yawn, "I got to get some sleep I been on my feet for ages." She fell on my bed and went to sleep. Suki sat next to her and started combing Di Di's hair.

Crystal called out.

"William I assume you heard everything?"

Pinstripes came in crimson faced barely controlling the anger in his voice.

"I was going through the kitchen accounts with the cook. He scanned a case of steaks in the freezer which has gone missing."

Crystal asked him, "Is he a good cook?"

"Yes and he knows it. That's why he steals groceries. He is testing the corruption level I allow to keep good help. I have zero tolerance. A case of aged steaks now then the next thing I will be fighting for is the silver utensils."

Crystal asked.

"How do you know it's the cook who ripped you off?"

"I don't care if he is guilty or not, it is his kitchen. Every item coming in and going out has to be accounted on the ledger. He is responsible."

"So who is winning?" Crystal asked.

"I am. The case of steaks turned up. The cook found the steaks in the poultry freezer. For good measure he fired a dishwasher. The poor Yugoslav didn't understand what hit. I found the Yugoslav a job in the Sixth Season Restaurant chain, Ying and Yang balance is reached by me."

"Was the Yugoslav guilty?"

"Aren't we getting slow Madam. It's the cook's kitchen, he hires and fires low level help. I have no idea if she was guilty or not. He has to inform me when he fires somebody, but I seldom interfere."

Crystal laughed. "Sometimes the cook is right."

I listened to William with a professional ear. I thought his account books must be easy to certify. Crystal opened a built in closet and pulled out a robe. She wrapped it around herself covering her see through nightgown. There was an awkward silence.

William yawned.

"Madam before I go to bed I would like to show you the account books for the last quarter. The computer is in the conference room."

Crystal looked at him pointedly. He in turn shifted his eyes toward sleeping Di Di. Silent communication passed between them. She said,

"Very well William lead the way." She grabbed my arm and pulled me along.

Pinstripes turned around and said.

"I am sure Mr. Goodwin will be bored by dry numbers."

"He is my husband and he is coming along." Crystal said with a touch of anger in her voice.

"He is not your husband madam." William snapped back.

"What makes you think that William?"

"Not even you would put your new husband in a guestroom."

I laughed and so did Crystal, but William stood there, looking grim. Crystal started pulling my sleeve again. "Joseph is a Certified Public Accountant and he is coming along. Lead the way William."

I couldn't quite understand why but Williams's attitude changed toward me from hostility to acceptance. We walked to a room with a big coat of arms on the door. There were a couple of animals on it plus Hebrews lettering and something in Latin. It was beautiful.

Crystal said.

"This is my conference room."

The room was empty.

Tweed touched a button on the wall and a Plexiglas contraption descendent from the ceiling; it had a large table and eight chairs and a pipe for cold air. We entered through a small door. The room was hot. Tweed said.

"The air conditioning will cool the room in a couple of minutes. This room is bug proof. I spent five million dollars developing it. I thought there would be a market for a totally bug proof room. Alas the price was too high for the government. I sold a couple of them privately but at a loss."

Crystal said.

"My, poor William, my uncle's bastard son. My Uncle was flamingly gay but one day he fell of the wagon and right into a stylish Brazilian debutante. Nine moths later there was a healthy baby boy."

"The debutante and her parents expected marriage but my uncle denied paternity. The debutante was aching for a court battle but her parents declined. They realized her life would be miserable, because unlike most gay men my uncle despised women and would have enjoyed dragging her reputation through the dirt. Instead they put William in a basket and handed him to my uncle's butler. The girl and her parent's moved back to Brazil.

"Uncle William had the baby's genes tested. It turned out the baby was ninety nine percent his stock. He handed the baby to the housekeeper and saw William Jr. once a year on Uncle William's own birthday."

"When I was born, seven years later, William Jr. was very happy. He spent more time in our house than is his. When I was two I followed him around like a caboose after an engine. When I was ten I was madly in love with him. But he kept his distance, because he taught I asked too many pointed questions about sex. I don't know if it's in the genes or what but William is gay as his father. Unlike his father, William adores women, and he prefers his sexual activities to be private as possible."

I asked.

"Speaking of private parts William was Crystal a boy at any time? She told me that she was a boy whom her mother turned into a girl?"

"That story. I don't know how many suitors she turned away with that story. This is the true story. When Crystal was eight she asked her mother why she didn't have something sticking out like me. Her mother cruelly told her that she used to have one but she had it cut it off, because she liked girls better. When I found out what an idiotic thing my aunt said I took Crystal to a therapist who after ten sessions came to the conclusion that there was no damage. She told me, Crystal thought mummy played a big joke on her. Crystal in turn played a big trick on mommy by making believe she was a boy for a couple of months. But mummy didn't seem to care one-way-or-another."

"I wish I could have seen therapist when I was eight. When my father found out I was gay he threw me out of the house."

His parting shot, said in a thunderous voice.

"You bloody fool I wanted grandchildren." Then he marched out of the room on six inch spikes.

"A couple of days later I wanted to tell him that if he wanted grandchildren he could have them. I have nothing against women. But before I could talk to him he died in a balloon accident that also killed Crystal's father." William had tears in his eyes. He was all choked up. Crystal continued the story for him.

"My uncle's will left William Jr. in my mothers care until he was twenty one. The will ordered my mother to train William to be a steward of her estate. He said from what he had seen of his son he will need a job to fall back on. He left William five hundred million dollars to be paid out when William turned sixty years old. William would forfeit the inheritance if he borrowed against the capital. He left William two ways to receive the inheritance before he reached sixty. If William fathered kids he would receive a hundred million with the birth of each child."

"How come I don't hear the steps of little feet in this palace? Hundred million is a hell of a lot of incentive even if you're gay. Viagra helps everybody." I said laughing.

Crystal said.

"That's what I keep telling him Joseph but he took the second option. If William made twenty million dollars in new technology in five years he could have the whole five hundred million dollars."

"William senior's foundation gives William five million dollars seed money once every five years. He can't carry the projects over to the next five years. If there is any money left over at the end of five years it is forfeited. If two million is left over at the end of five years then William receives three million more for the next five years. This setup can go on until William turns sixty when he gets the whole bundle with interest no matter what."

"William can do anything with the five million but there is no five hundred million until his gray. When William got his first five million he blew it in three years. He was broke so he came to work for me. Mother just died in a car accident and I needed somebody I could trust to manage my affairs.

"My mother lived in a royal fantasy so she trained William to be a real royal steward. I became the haunted princes and he became the loyal steward."

"I hope he never wins the prize but I would like to hear the patter of little feet around the palace William. In the last ten years he has been funding bright inventors but no go so far. William is brilliant and loving but he smothered me. I had nothing to do accept sign contracts. One day I got sick of William. I went to New York and bought into a rundown club known as One Plus One Equals Three. You know the rest Joseph."

William said with a belly laugh.

"The way this invention thing is going I will have to opt out for the family trip. You know Joseph I never thought of Viagra even though my problem is what it cures. I go limp whenever I get near a woman. It's bloody embarrassing when a woman wants old fido and it won't perform. I am in analyses. My therapist, is sick of it, but I can't get past that my mother abandoning me to a flaming drag queen of a father. The sexual screws in my head are loose Joseph."

"Enough of the family gossip let's get down to business. Number one problem is Cathy Chin. If she is out to avenge her brother then we are in hot water. We can't go to police although that is what I want to do. If the Swede is an example of the fidelity of my employees then all we have is the three us to fight Cathy Chin. I still can't believe Freddie allowed Di Di on the grounds. I am seriously thinking of firing him." Crystal said with flaming anger in her voice. "FBI badge or not he should have asked for a warrant at least."

"Don't be hasty. He is a very good groundskeeper and driver. Di Di came armed to the teeth against Freddie, after she met with Robert Park, the Toyota family's chauffer. He disarmed her without breaking any laws. As it stands even if he did break some law she likes him enough to forget about it." William said.

"Baloney" I said, "Freddie was scared when she showed him the FBI badge. You can stop putting us on William. He can't be counted on when something illegal is involved."

"That's how I see it too William; Joseph and I have gone through some scary times in the last week. We don't want a weak link when we face Cathy."

"Here is the real story" William said, "He was not scared but he knew he might be facing an assault charge for crippling the Korean driver. Soon as he opened the door Di Di accused him of attempted murder of the Korean driver."

"If you ask Di Di she will tell you she forced her way in but the truth is Freddie let her in while making believe he was blocking the way. He was screwing around with her waiting for me to come down and take charge. I am sure DI Di likes him. She won't run to report him for beating up the limo driver but it might cost us some money. Despite the fact that he didn't disable the tracking device on Korean's limousine I trust him, because it was my job to tell him to disable it."

"He is my man. I don't mean that in a sexual way Joseph. I mean I pay part of his salary out of my own money, because he drives me on my trysts out of the closet. He pays rent for the second cottage in the back and he is not allowed in the palace. He is very clever fellow within limits. He was hitting the bottle when I met him."

"He lost his previous position as a driver, because he was too big for the families new Mercedes. He is really too big to be a driver of most of our cars so I offered him the ground keeper's job. I pay him well for a groundskeeper."

"A few years ago I invested some of my five year allowance with an inventor who turned out to be a swindler. I threatened to sue him. He just laughed. I sent Freddie to talk him. He came back with a check that did not bounce. I used him for some minor things. This thing yesterday with the Korean driver was his first big job. All in all I'll give him ninety percent on performance. He also has a wife who is pregnant with twins. You will hear the sound of little feet in two months. As I said he is a good person to have around."

I said.

"I'll take your word for it William and I will hold you to it."

"I am glad you take my word for it Joseph, but it's none of your business what I do."

"It is my business. I held a man while Crystal poked his eyes out with a key, because he wasn't coming up with the information we needed. When Di Di called Peter Wong's Detective Agency in England he mentioned that I was on Cathy Chin's hit list."

"What we need is a plan that involves dirty work. Freddie won't do it, because his wife is pregnant and he won't jeopardize his green card." I spit out the words really angry. I had enough of Williams' bullshit.

"Yes you do have to do dirty work Joseph," William said calmly, "yes you do and I have a plan. We own a little insurance company in Taiwan and where there is insurance there is insurance fraud. When Happy Home Insurance suspects fraud it hires Good Luck Detection Service based in the Philippines. The Chinese family that owns the detective agency lived in the Philippines when it was still a Spanish colony. I will get them to set up a discreet twenty four hour surveillance of Cathy Chin. We will infiltrate the Buddhist Temple with a woman operator who will make friends with Cathy . . ."

Crystal and I both said it at the same time.

"No!"

I said.

"Don't let anyone close to her. She is in the security business. She will spot a ringer. She will turn our agent against us. She has a lot of money and money talks when you are in New York."

"Joseph you definitely have a problem with trust. Happy Home Insurance will hire Good Luck Detection Service. They will do as Happy Home Insurance instructs, because if they don't they will lose Happy Home Insurance as an account. Happy Home Insurance is the detective agencies number one red ribbon account. They won't screw us, because if we drop them in a public way all their high class clients will follow us. You know why Joseph, because I straightened them out two years ago.

"Happy Home Insurance started doing business in mainland China three years ago. We finally got all the permits to operate there. We wrote a lot of medium sized policies. The ink was hardly dry before we were hit with a string of fires. We sent Good Luck Detection Service to investigate. Their operators who were local Chinese stringers reported that all the fires were legit. We paid the claims just to show good will but the Chief Operating Officer of Happy Home Insurance jumped all over Good Luck Detection Service."

"Our COO pulled the account from Good Luck Detection Service and waited. Sure enough, the head of the family an eighty year old man, came from the Philippines. He brought with him seven men in wheel chairs. They all had broken backs. The old man said they had accidents while coming back from work in mainland China. "We gave your company seventy years of good service we will give you good service for another seventy years and then he left. I told our Chief Operating Officer to return the account to Good Luck Detection Service. I liked the old man's style."

Crystal asked with a bubbly laugh.

"How do you know he didn't find seven guys in a nursing home?"

"Crystal don't start getting suspicious on me. Joseph is bad enough. Every guy had a dossier in his lap with full biography and confession."

"OK, we will hire them." Crystal said laughing.

"No contact with Cathy. Make that clear to William, Crystal." I said.

"Big brothers don't screw around, my life is at stake." Crystal said rubbing her eyes as if she were crying.

William said dejected.

"OK Joseph, you and I work together. You know I can't understand how the hell you two got in to this mess. I viewed the tapes. I almost shit in my pants when Chin killed Brown."

"We actually met the son of bitch. He was really mean and his sister Cathy Chin is no better." Crystal said.

"This operation will run into millions Crystal!" William warned

They started bickering about money. I am an accountant so talk of money bores me unless it's on my ledger. I started looking at the monitors. It's amazing how many rooms and crannies this palace had. They had two cameras for the kitchen area alone. I looked at the room where Di Di and

Suki were supposed to be sleeping. Di Di was sleeping like a log but Suki wasn't there.

I snapped my finger at them and pointed at the monitor. William was slow on the uptake but Crystal yelled pointing to the monitor. "Let's see if she is in the bathroom." William said smugly. He took out a bunch of keys and put one of them in a lock on the table next to the monitors. Pictures of many different bathrooms replaced the images on the monitors. A lovely woman was taking a bath in the servant's quarter but the rest of them were empty.

"I think we will have to have a long talk about spying on the help's bathrooms. I see a nasty law suit if they find the cameras, William." Crystal said smugly.

"Don't be so noble dear if I didn't design the installation of those cameras in your New York home you would be dead without them." William said with anger in his voice.

"Touché, William, you got me so where the hell is Suki?"

"Let's check the garage. A picture of a large garage full of cars came on the screen. Yes, Suki is gone and so is my Bugatti. Before you start having fits Crystal it's not the one your mother died in. It's the latest model." William offered.

I asked. "How come we didn't hear the engine noise. And how did she get out? The big door is broken."

"The garage is sound proofed and the back door has one of those locks that can be opened from the inside without the key but not from the outside. But there is the video camera in the garage." Crystal said dejectedly.

"Yes there is one, and I have a DVD of the last twenty four hours." William said happily. He was in his element snooping on people.

He played around with the machine until he found Suki selecting the car, turning the car key and pulling up to the back gate where she opened the gate and drove out. To our surprise Freddie the chauffeur a little later closed the back gate.

"He is fired," Crystal said simply, while hugging herself.

"Don't be like that, Crystal. He just found the back gate open and closed it, there is nothing wrong with that." William said alarmed.

"What about the fact that he did not notice that the Bugatti was stolen." Crystal said with spice in her voice.

"Suki closed the garage door after herself. You saw it on the video Crystal. Don't be so hard on me, I run a good operation for you. There is nothing we can do about Suki without attracting undo attention to us so lets all go to sleep and see what tomorrow brings." William chirped with hope in his voice . . . .

I said, mournfully, Di Di is going to hit the roof when she wakes up."

"Screw her! Suki took a three hundred thousand dollar car. Not that I mind, she could total the car, as long as she comes back safely." Crystal said with tears in her eyes.

"If you call the cops they will find her in an hour. A car like that stands out like a sore thumb." I said hopefully.

"William! Is the satellite tracking device in the car?" Crystal asked suddenly.

"No! That's the car, I use when I step out of the closet, dear." William said defensively. He had the nerve to sound indignant.

I said to nobody, "now it makes sense why Freddie didn't make a big fuss when he saw the Bugatti leave. He probably thought the boss was on the prowl again."

"How far, are you in the closet, William?" Crystal asked while she was playing with the monitors.

"I think I am pretty gay. I am thinking of a transsexual operation."

Crystal and I said at the same time. "Are you thinking of having your penis cut of?"

William pulled himself up to his full five feet seven inches and said with a tear in his eye.

"I will sacrifice it for love."

"For Freddie?" Crystal asked ready to accept the romance.

"For Freddie?" William said with contempt in his voice, "he is my driver."

"No, my love is a Greek Adonis. He is a gigolo, on the Bahamas Cruise Lines. He is a little crazy. He loves older women. I offered him money, but when I talk to him about man to man love, he thinks I am joking. He slaps, me on the back, and starts talking about mature women. I love him madly. So I have been thinking, if I have the operation, he will have to accept me as a rich old dame. He is twenty eight and gorgeous. He hits on women who are in their late fifties and early sixties. He is not very successful. He is too eager."

"I have, no pride, I'll take him." Di Di's loud voice was coming through the camera monitoring her room.

William struck a pose and said. "You will never get him, Bitch."

With a flourish William, pushed a button on the console, and all the monitors went blank.

"That should fix her. Let her talk to me now, taking Ricardo from me, indeed."

As I expected five minutes later there was banging on the oak doors. William went into a tizzy.

"I am, not letting her in. Let her stew."

Crystal got up and opened the door for Di Di. She looked around and laughed hilariously.

"What have we got here the little yellow submarine?"

"Don't be, so proud of yourself Madam, you are not the first one to make that joke," William said glaring at Di Di.

"What is the name of my new boyfriend?" Di Di asked laughing, "William ignored her, while tapping his foot on the floor, a mile a minute.

Crystal said.

"I think his name is Ricardo. Did you hear that Suki took off in William's Bugatti?"

"I heard it, although I thought I was dreaming. Ricardo, is that his lovely name, William?"

"Maybe we can have a threesome." Di Di said half seriously.

"Give me a garbage pail so I can throw up." William said undulating like a snake.

I said to William, "It is not such a bad idea to introduce Di Di to Ricardo. She may say nice things about you to him."

"Hell no, not that man eater, next thing he will be traveling to Japan, and I'll lose his friendship forever."

"This is a lot of bullshit, if you don't mind my saying so, what about Suki, Di Di?" Crystal asked fidgeting with her gown.

"We can ask the police to locate the car. I gather from the look on your face Joseph that is out of the question. Then you figure out how to find her." William said feeling dejected that no one else came to support him.

"She, generally goes where there are Japanese. Miami, is a great place to find Japanese, if you know where to look, like the yellow pages. Tomorrow the Swede and I will hunt for her. I tried calling her but she has her cell turned off. Meanwhile what kind of idiot spies on a person and forgets to turn off the two way mikes?" Di Di asked.

William turned beet red and said, "It was a mistake on the parts order when we installed the mikes. By the time I realized what was happening the two way mikes were built in to the wall. It would have cost a hundred thousand to remove them. I was running over budget so I left them in. If Joseph wouldn't have messed around with the controls the mikes wouldn't have been turned on."

I was about to say, "I didn't touch a thing." But Crystal interrupted. "Is the servant's quarter wired like this? Am I facing a lawsuit down the line?"

"Don't get excited Crystal I had the wiring ripped out of the servant's quarters. No slipups, just one way mikes."

"Good, now pull out the junk from rest of the house. I will sign the work order tomorrow." Crystal said bored but you could skate on the chill in her voice.

William said gruffly. "Your mother authorized it."

"Don't start lying William. My mother fought my father when he installed a visible video camera to keep an eye on my nanny. She would never have authorized this monstrosity. The way I see it you made this plastic monster and started snooping on everybody."

"Starting tonight it is going in mothballs. The door gets locked and no one uses it. The normal surveillance areas like the kitchens the doors and the like will be done by visible cameras with red lights indicating that the cameras are on."

William turned purple. His chest was heaving so hard he couldn't talk. He yanked open a drawer and produced a butcher knife he stood above Crystal menacingly. Without getting out of her chair Crystal kicked William in the balls with both her knees.

William fell back, howling, stabbing himself accidentally in the arm. He passed out from the sight of his own blood. It was a nasty cut, because the knife hit a vein. I used my belt as a tourniquet to stop the bleeding. We sat around William watching a small trickle blood hit the floor. William was white from shock. Crystal's toes inched toward the puddle of blood. I kicked her foot away and hissed. "AIDS, my baby, AIDS."

"So what are we going to do about him? I can't allow emergency services into this fish bowl." Crystal asked in a bad mood.

We carried William to one of the guest rooms and put him in a chair then called 911.

The EMS guys arrived and took charge. One of them said. "So he tried to commit suicide."

Our silence set the EMS guys back but they recovered fast, and told us not to worry William would recover but he would need a shrink, if he didn't have one already. William came out his swoon and started sputtering that he did not try suicide. But it was too late they bundled him on a gurney and took off. Crystal went along with them.

Di Di walked back to the guestroom with me.

"You got your money Joseph?"

"Yes, I didn't have a chance to thank you properly."

"Why don't you take your money and leave? These people are really crazy."

"I thought about leaving Di Di but I am hung up on Suki and Crystal. We have become a twisted threesome. I can't get away from them."

"Suki seems to have gotten away from you two, very nicely." Di Di sniffed. Wiping her eyes she said.

"I want to meet William's beautiful Greek. Joseph help me and I will throw you candy kisses for the rest of our happy life."

"Sure why not Di Di, I'll find out which liner he sails on, but William might kill you, I mean it's pretty serious, he is thinking of a sex change operation to please Ricardo."

"He doesn't have to know. You know what I mean?"

"Yes, I'll get you a photo when William comes back from the emergency room. I will suggest a cruise to the Bahamas. I will tell him Crystal and I want to meet the love of his life. Crystal and I could use the rest anyway. Meanwhile, you and the Swede search for Suki, as you planned."

"Imagine that a guy in his twenties and all he wants is money for his loving and on top of that he *likes* to make it with middle age women what a gem. Sorry William! But that man is mine." Di Di cackled to herself out loud.

I went back to my room took a shower and hit the bed naked and slept until a cat scratched my back. I awoke with a start. The cat turned out to be Crystal and she was scratching my ass with her long nails. It wasn't sexy, it hurt, but I made an attempt, to pull her under me.

She simply said, "I can't do it now Joseph. I spent six hours with William the crybaby. He lost a lot of blood and on top of that he nicked a bone in his arm. It hurt William oh so much. I am going to sleep now."

She conked out. I thought bitterly I'll never screw her. I put on my boxers and went to the kitchen to get some food. The fat cook blocked my way. I told him I was hungry. He offered me breakfast that I ate greedily in the servants dining area. I asked one of the maids to show me where William lived. She blushed crimson as she pointedly looked at my boxers. I looked down, I am afraid I was hanging out.

William had a nice little apartment in the guest part of the castle. He was sitting propped up by pillows on his bed. I didn't waste time, I told him I wanted to meet his flame.

"I proposed a Bahamas holiday. He looked at me suspiciously. "You are not gay are you?" I said "no" with heavy emphasis on the letter "n" to convince him.

"I got to meet this guy after all you are going to have a sex change operation for him. You are giving up the possibilities of children at hundred million a child."

"Ok, we will go sailing but that Japanese bitch is not coming along. We will make it a regular holiday. I will bring the cook and a nurse."

"Now go away Joseph. I got plans to make . . . I got a closet full of designers clothing to wear. Shoo, Shoo go away Joseph. I got plans to make. I think I will take the whole household and as a grand finale I will have my operation and metamorphose into a social butterfly on the ship. You know Joseph Crystal was quite nice to me in the emergency room. She may pay for the whole party if I ask her sweetly."

He grabbed my hand feverishly. "Joseph you have to help me to convince her to go along with the adventure. A word from you and she will pay for turning me from chrysalis to a butterfly."

"How much do you have in mind?" I asked suspiciously.

"Two or three million dollars at most," William said excitedly squeezing my hand with his limp hand.

"I will help you William but you have to draw up a proposition that we can present to Crystal."

"No, that's too dry I want to appeal to her romantically. By the way about the children not that it's your business I had my sperm frozen. I could have hundreds of children if I want to. There is no prohibition in the will against it. I finally figured out how to screw dear daddy."

"Ok, William you have brains, I thought you were blowing all that money on a romance that may not work out. By the way do you have pictures of Ricardo? I like to see the man."

William eagerly produced ten developer's envelopes with pictures from under his pillow. All the pictures were of his love, Ricardo in the pool Ricardo in the gym etc.. Ricardo had a magnificent head on a small body. His craggy face could be considered handsome but his muscles were more like sinews. I couldn't see cutting off my private parts for the fellow. William volunteered that his last name was Ricardo too. Ricardo Ricardo was in hundreds of pictures. I palmed one of them. William was so involved looking at the photographs that I could have take ten without him noticing. I told William he made a good choice. He beamed and shook my hand. I left the room promising to help him with Crystal.

No one was around so in my boredom I explored the Palace. The architecture was bizarre but the Persian rugs and the tapestry were magnificent. I own a couple of valuable rugs but compared to these they were rags. The furniture was Louie the Sun Kings period. Lots of money went into this place but Crystal treats it as some kind of outhouse.

My attention was distracted by the sound of tip tap on the marble. I turned around and to my astonishment I was facing a geisha in full regalia. She was beautiful exotic and her demeanor gave me an erection. I only had boxer shorts on so it was difficult to hide it. She giggled and hit me with her fan that got rid of the erection. "Sorry Joseph but I can't take advantage of your excited state, because Suki would dump me if she found out but you are nice looking."

I said astonished. "I know by your voice it's you Di Di, but your body is out of a dream."

"I going to see the Swede, I think little exotica will entice him. I will have to charm his wife too. We will travel in Japanese circles and I will dress this way. I am getting Suki back. A Geisha gets respect and a lot of help. How do you think Ricardo will react to me?"

"He will be floored. Here is a photo of him and he lives on the Bahaman Leisure Lines."

"He never gets off the ship unless there is a lady involved. He gambles just enough to show bravura to the ladies. According to William, Ricardo is frugal, so don't expect flowers."

Di Di hugged the picture to her bosom and whispered.

"I am going to have fun on this damn trip after all." She tapped me lightly with her fan.

"I am going to see, the Swede now, then we will go to Miami, the yellow pages has some promising leads, we should be back in a couple of days." She tiptoed away on wooden clogs.

I thought William my boy you have a serious competitor. I started laughing until my side hurt. I went back to my room and flopped down next to Crystal and fell asleep.

A week passed. We heard from Di Di every evening but she had no luck finding Suki. Despite my misgivings we called the police and reported the Bugatti stolen. The police reassured us that it won't be found. Cars like that end up in a shipping container heading for South America in no time.

Middle of the third week Suki showed up driving the Bugatti. She wore a silk poncho like thing that covered her arms and legs. She wouldn't look us in the eye. She walked as if she was in a dream. Crystal hugged her happily but Suki's hands stayed at her side not responding.

Suki's face neck and hands were filthy. She had dirt under her cracked nails. She smelled of Clorox. Crystal told me to pick her up and carry her to the master bathroom, in Crystal's quarters, the bath was a little pool in the shape of a half shell and everything metal was solid gold. I turned to leave but Suki became animated and grabbed me and asked me pitifully to stay. Crystal pulled off Suki's poncho and stepped back stunted. Suki's naked body was covered with black and blue marks. Some of the marks were yellowing with age others looked fresh.

I asked, "What the hell happened to you?" but Crystal put her finger on my lips and said that I should put Suki in the tub. I did and sat on the floor cross legged and watched as Crystal washed Suki with a washcloth and mild soap.

Suddenly Suki shouted. "I hate the son of bitch. If he would have whipped me before sex I might have loved him, but he hit me for not cleaning properly, I hate him. He is a Puritan who does not believe in sex but he beat me for everything else. If there was so much as a wrinkle in a shirt I ironed I got it with a whip. He is a coke head."

"He had people over and I had to serve them and if I made a mistake he hit me in front of the whole company. At first I enjoyed the humiliation then I got sick of it and started getting even. One bitch got furious when I put a ton of hot peppers in her Bloody Mary. The Poor darling almost choked on the drink. She told Master Hugo, "better get rid of this slave she is getting to uppity." I didn't like the way she said "get rid off" I decided to leave. It is a big house on the ocean front. On some nights boats without lights would come in the slip for an hour or two then leave.

One night Master Hugo was complaining to his houseboy that he was stuck with a load of coke, because the guy who was supposed to buy it over dosed on heroin. He had three shipments coming in that week and he was short on cash. I jumped on the opportunity. I looked him in the eye and told him I had a friend who had money and would buy the coke. He slapped me for looking him in the eye and then asked. "How much money?" I said, "I bet enough for a hundred kilos." He said that's a million five hundred thousand. You think you can handle that?" I said yes, eagerly.

"In gratitude he gave me a beating and said if I failed he would drown me in the ocean. He gave me the car keys and here I am."

"How in hell did you run into this guy?" Crystal asked incredulously.

When I left here I drove to Miami. It was pretty late the only Japanese place I found open was an all night Sushi place. The Sushi chef was a young guy with red dyed hair. We started talking and things got hot. I told him I would blow his little dick. Usually this makes Japanese boys hot to screw.

They all want to prove how big they are even though I tell them size doesn't matter."

"You like big dicks?" The sushi boy asked me coldly.

"I said yes, not knowing where he was leading,"

He gave me a card and said.

"Go there and you will see a man with the biggest penis in the world."

"Somehow it didn't feel right, I told him I was not that interested Americans, I would rather be with him."

He smiled and came over and picked me up and threw me out of the restaurant. I got up from the grass and drove to the address on the card. I thought after the experience with the Japanese kid this guy better have the biggest member in the world. A naked Philippine servant opened the door. I looked at his crotch it looked normal sized. I gave him the Japanese kid's card. From deep in the house a gruff voice shouted. "Who the hell is it at this hour?"

"A bitch the sushi boy sent." Answered the houseboy shoving me, in to the room where this big mouthed guy was in a whirlpool, naked. I looked at his crotch. His penis looked unusually small but fat.

"Not impressed by me are you? You came to see, the biggest dick in the world, right?" he pushed a button on a remote control and a movie of two elephants fornicating appeared on a wide screen TV. I had to admit the bull elephant's penis was largest thing I ever saw.

"How would you like to sleep with that?"

Without thinking I said, "Are you out of your mind? It would kill me."

"The first thing you have to learn that I am never out of my mind."

He got out of the bath and picked up a bamboo stick and beat me unconscious. When I woke up I found myself chained to the foot of the Filipino's bed. The houseboy was up and puttering around the room dressed in a towel around his waist. When he saw me conscious he simply said.

"The boss has the biggest dick in the world. If he asks you say he is the biggest you ever saw far too big for you to take. If you say it as if you mean it he won't hit you too much."

I didn't believe the houseboy. I thought he was setting me up for a beating. I mean no self-respecting man would believe such an obvious lie. I told the houseboy the boss showed me the elephant penis after that no one in his right mind would believe that a human's dick is bigger. The houseboy gave me a stinging slap.

"Who said he was in his right mind, when you stepped in to this house, you became a slave. You can start your service by brushing his bathroom with a toothbrush. If you do a good job I will give you a normal size brush and hot water. If you do a bad job he boss will beat you mercilessly. If you do a good job he will beat you but not as badly. He is a sadist. He likes his slaves to beg for mercy so do plenty of crying and begging. I am not a sadist, but I will give you a beating, if you do something that reflects on me badly. You get bread and water today, three normal meals tomorrow, the next day back to bread and water, and following day regular meals, and so on and so on. If you make too many mistakes you just get bread and water for a week besides the beatings."

"That night the boss inspected my work every time he found something wrong he gave me a slap. He found a lot of things wrong. When he finished inspecting he got undressed. He stood front of the picture of the elephants and he asked me who had the biggest prick in the world. Without thinking I said the elephant did. He howled like a banshee and grabbed me by the neck and forced his penis which was very

142

short but had unusual girth down my throat. I couldn't breath I started fighting him but he slapped me with his fist when I moved. I passed out for lack of air. When I came too he asked me who had the biggest penis. I told him, begging for mercy, that he did.

Things eased up a bit. The boss would beat me whenever he saw me but the houseboy started warning me when the boss was around giving me a chance to hide. I was terrified. I would have cut my own wrist if the drug deal didn't come up. I want to cry but I am all out of tears. Hold me Joseph. I need to feel someone who loves me."

I held her and combed her hair with my fingers. She started sobbing quietly. Crystal kissed her on the cheek, Suki cheered up and said laughing.

"At least I got your car back, Crystal."

"Hell with the car Suki lets call the police department. Lets get him arrested and that Japanese bastard who sent you to him."

Suki stiffened in my arms.

"No," she said determinedly. "I want the hundred kilos of cocaine, besides he has contacts in the Miami police department. I would get arrested and killed in jail."

I told her he was probably lying about the police to scare her. She told me that Master Hugo never lied. At one of his parties there were two detectives as guest of honor. One of them gave me a beating when I dropped avocado dip on his pants.

Where are we going to get that much money on a weekend? We went to William's apartment. William was snoring loudly. Suki kicked his bed which scared William. He pulled a derringer from under his pillow. When he recognized Suki he put the gun down and said.

"Where the hell have you been daughter of Nippon? Di Di is going out her mind looking for you. Did you bring the Bugatti back?"

"Yes, I have the car and from now on it is my car and as for Di Di she is the last person I want to see today, tomorrow or ever."

I was about to come to Di Di's defense but Crystal interrupted me.

"William do you have a million five hundred thousand in the house?"

"No, Crystal darling I only have a hundred thousand in petty cash and your bank manager is in Aruba. No telephones in his villa so we can't get in touch with him. You will have to wait till Tuesday when he returns to get that kind of money off the books. I assume it has something do with Suki coming back. Why are you black and blue Suki?"

"Master Hugo," Suki said sobbing.

"Ho, Ho, you met him and you are still around that is something new. Usually his slaves end up in a whorehouse in Mexico or Brazil. He is a big guy in the Coconut Grove section of Miami. He is the roughest of the rough trade. It is rumored that he kills a homosexual man or woman to celebrate his birthday." William told them without emotion.

"If you know all this, why don't you go to the police and have him arrested." I asked not bothering to hide my anger.

"He has the law in his back pocket. He is the biggest drug dealer in Florida. From coke, to heroin, to grass, he deals with them all and the law gets a golden share of his profit. Some people say he made a deal with the Devil. Gay people hang around him like moths around a flame. Whenever the Swede and I see him in the Grove we leave the bar and go somewhere else. In his social life he is bent as a crooked nail but when it comes to business he has a sterling reputation. Whatever, you guy are going to do, please keep the Swede and I out of it."

Suki started sobbing quietly, "he will get me if I don't show up,"

"He probably will but then you didn't have to steal my car and leave in the middle of the night. You put on a big show, because of Di Di's indiscretion but Di Di didn't do anything wrong. She touched Freddie's crotch, because she was scared of him. Even a selfish little bitch like you should have understood that," William turned red in the face as he talked.

Suki shrunk under the barrage of nasty words.

"You are right William, I will try to make up with her when she comes back home. You see William when I saw her touch his crotch and giggle, something snapped in me. It's like watching your parents make love in front of you. It feels yucky. She is my milk mother."

"What does that mean?" William asked puzzled.

"She is my wet nurse."

"Ok, she is like a parent. How was I to know?" William replied mollified.

A smirk passed over Suki's face far too fast for William to notice. I thought to myself Suki learned a few tricks mollifying Master Hugo, I didn't blame her, I felt sorry for her. Her innocence was gone with the wind.

I had no doubt Hugo could find us, he had the Bugatti's license number, from that he could get the address of the castle.

I turned to Crystal and told her I would put up the million and half dollars if she would guarantee to replace the money if things went sour. Both women jumped on me and kissed me all over my face. Even William got in the act and gave me a brotherly kiss on my forehead. I realized after I gave them the money that Crystal didn't promise to replace the money if it was lost.

Suki called Master Hugo, he demanded her address, but she refused to give to him. He told her it didn't mater someone followed her home. Sitting around the speakerphone we almost lost our courage. He and Suki made arrangement for the exchange. We planned to force Hugo to come to our county where William had pull with the police. But that was no go from the start. He dictated to Suki and she crumbled like a good slave.

We were to meet in a garage downtown Miami. The top floor of the garage was under repair and not used. The exchange would take place up there. We were told to park our car on the fourth floor then walk up to the fifth where he would be waiting. I put the speakerphone on hold and told Suki, "No way, we are not walking around with a million and a half dollars. You tell him we will meet him on the top floor. We will have a white van with three yellow ribbons on the bumper.

They will load the product in our car while Master Hugo counts the money. She repeated what I said. Hugo became suspicious, "Is somebody giving you advice?" Suki finally lost her temper and shouted on the top of her lung, "who the hell do you think is putting up the million and the half dollars. He needs assurance that he won't lose his money to a hijacker."

"Tell him not worry I clear that much in a week. How many people are you bringing?" I signaled three. Suki told him three. We decided to do it next day at four in the afternoon.

"What the hell are we going to do with a million and a half worth of coke? William do you have customers in the gay world?"

"Yeah, I could sell a couple of ounces without trouble." William replied seriously.

"How long?"

He said. "I could unload three or four ounces in a week." William bragged.

"At that rate it will take ten years to unload the crap. We have to do better than that."

Suki and Crystal were talking in hushed tones at the end of the table while William and I were bickering. I couldn't hear what they were saying but Crystal was forcing something on Suki. Suki put on a brave front then collapsed visibly her head bobbing up and down in agreement.

"I am taking a shotgun tomorrow. I am not getting robbed. Our darling Suki is not that sure of Hugo's honesty when it comes to slaves. Crystal proclaimed, "I am telling you Suki William is going to strap you if you don't come back to our side."

William gave a wicked grin. "It will be my pleasure Suki dearest. Million and a half is a lot of money and a lot of pain for you for bringing this predicament on us. Nobody knew I lived here. The car is registered in a dead letter address and I take different routes when I come home from Miami. After all daughter of Nippon I live in the closet. Now the male whores, who will surely hear about this thanks to you, will want big money for the act. Yeah, darling I'll whip your ass without mercy."

"Good, do it William, but I don't think a milksop like you has it in you. Don't be surprised if I will kick you in the balls. I kicked Hugo real hard but he just laughed. The son-of-a-bitch wears an armored cup. I am going to listen to Crystal, because I want to protect Joseph's money." She turned toward me and said. "You could do something to protect me Joseph. I went trough hell. I am slowly coming back to myself."

I told her to call Di Di. She did it with lot of hesitation. I went over to her and kissed her on the lips. She pulled back but a second later she came back for another one. She cried heavy tears on my chest. I held her lightly. Her whole body was trembling. Finally a giant tremor shook her body. She kissed me and pushed me away smiling. "I am calling Di Di."

Suki called Di Di. There was a lot of talk in Japanese. At one point Suki dropped the phone and turned to us white faced. "Di Di killed the Japanese boy who sent me to Hugo."

The Swede held him while Di Di questioned the sushi boy. The boy told them about the biggest penis in the world but he was too scared tell her Hugo's address. She got pissed and stabbed him in the heart with a long hairpin. Freddie threw the boy under the counter then pushed Di Di to the floor and drove off with the limousine cursing.

Lucky for Di Di, it was a slow night in the restaurant, she told the help as she was leaving laughing that the boy got so excited by her bawdy stories that he went to the bathroom to do you know what. She went to a motel and stripped her Geisha outfit and put on western clothing.

She rented a car and she will be here in the morning. She told me to tell Freddie, not to worry, because she had a long talk with the owner of the sushi joint.

She told him if he talked about Freddie and her then she will tell them about the biggest penis in the world and Hugo. The owner was apologetic the way only a Japanese can be under pressure, he said, "the boy is alligator meat. Nobody knows anything."

One of the surveillance TV screens gave out a buzz. The limousine entered through the back gate. The Swede parked the car in the garage and headed for the castle.

"He can't come in here," William said childishly, "it is off limits for outside help."

"It doesn't matter lets hear what he has to say." Crystal hissed.

Unexpectedly one of the bookcase's opened and in walked the big man. He was agitated, his knees were shaking, his voice trembled,

"I need the thirty thousand dollars you owe me boss and I am quitting as of right now. I am not taking a stitch of furniture just some clothing and my wife and I are gone." Surrounded by calm people he started relaxing.

His nervous crossed eyes rested on Suki.

"So here you are. Did you know that crazy milk mother of yours killed a kid, because he wouldn't tell her where he sent you?"

"Yes, and you bugged out and left her there." Suki answered cruelly.

"If you want to know the truth I almost hit her but I got control of myself and left fast. I figured she would workout something with the owner's wife. The sushi joint's owner's wife is something special in the sex slave trade, my being there just complicated things, for Di Di. I stood out like a sore thumb. Everybody is very calm here, so I gather Di Di called."

William replied. "She did call a couple of minutes ago. Your precious ass is saved, the boy is alligator meat. What about this thirty thousand you are not trying to blackmail me Freddie?"

"No way boss, I just want six months severance pay as you promised, when you hired me, I can't take the pressure, I need a vacation and a new job."

"I will take care of this William," Crystal interrupted, "I will pay you ninety thousand dollars. I assume you make sixty thousand dollars a year, that is a year and a half pay. You go and retrain and practice calming yoga for eighteen months then return to work. William with his idiotic plan to become a woman needs a bodyguard and you are it Freddie. Bring me my business checkbook William."

"I am afraid mum, that it's going to be the thirty thousand, and I quit. As a matter of fact if you don't want to pay the thirty thousand then so be it I quit anyway." Freddie said getting up from the chair.

"Freddie you haven't got a choice. All the workers in the Japanese restaurant will swear that you killed the boy. William needs a bodyguard and straight company. Please take the eighteen months to pull yourself together and come back to work. I will increase your salary to eighty thousand a year with a nice New Year bonus. I think that is fair."

"I can't do it mum."

"Let me put it another way. You leave here and you will fall off the wagon and as a drunk you will start babbling about your past life. You may let it slip that this Japanese broad killed a boy with a pair of hatpins. Are you getting my drift Freddie?" Crystal asked him roughly.

"It is true but I haven't had a drink since I started working for, William. I have a feeling I am making a devil's bargain. I will take the money and return in eighteen months. I am going Tibet. I did a terrible thing to that Korean limousine driver. I have to clean my soul."

"And I have the feeling that I am in one of those boring Swedish movies." Crystal laughed.

"Would you like cash or a check?"

"Check Mum, I want to pay taxes." Crystal wrote him a check.

Freddie bowed before the company and went out through the bookcase.

"I didn't know Freddie knew about that secret entrance. That wasn't meant to be an entrance it was meant to be a rapid exit. Thanks for taking care Freddie, Crystal." William said wiping tears from his eyes with his knuckles.

"While we are at it William, I will foot the bill for your transformation, within reason. No more than two million dollars and renting the whole ship is out. It attracts too many thieves."

"I want the whole ship." William replied doing a perfect Judy Garland imitation.

We laughed hysterically.

"I will buy you a hundred first class accommodations for those who are first class and three hundred in tourist class for a ten day cruise. I will pay for setting up the surgery and the doctor bills unless your medical insurance pays for it. I think it will cost more than two million but what the hell William you will be a lovely woman. I thought your chest was getting fat but you must be taking hormone shots."

"You noticed Crystal. You noticed WoW the hormone shots are working. I will get implants to give my breast nice shape. I'll do it a couple of weeks before the cruise so I can show my breast to the adoring crowd on the ship, Wow, Wow, Wow." He kept saying Wow as he sashayed around the room. For a moment we were totally relaxed and entertained. Out of the corner of my eye I watched William closely for signs of fear or duplicity but there was nothing, he was totally in to it and enjoying the attention.

Then as if by magic he was back as the manager of Crystal's Palace straight as a reed. "I will tell the chef to prepare supper, meanwhile we could have sandwiches, in the tearoom. I suggest resting as much as you can, because tomorrow with Hugo could prove very hectic." Crystal and Suki smiled at each other. The two little cats are going to eat a canary I thought.

The tearoom was a terrarium full of tropical plants. Humid but cool. The chef brought the food with ingratiating smile on his fat face.

"Cucumber sandwiches Madam? The gardener just picked them fresh off the vine."

To my surprise she ordered William to tell the cook that she didn't care for the English tea sandwiches. A good old fashioned hamburger on a whole wheat bun and pickle and tomato will do."

The cook gave William a poisonous look.

"What will you drink madam?" the red faced chef asked.

"William tell the cook, never mind, don't tell him anything. Chef what are you doing here? Your domain is the kitchen and unless I call for you there is no reason for you to be in the living quarters."

The chef's color turned from red to purple then to ashen white.

"Yes Madam," the chef said backing out.

"You can leave the sandwiches. They are quite good."

The Chef gave her a screw you look and left without the tray.

"Is that enough of a boost in your battles with the cook William?"

"Yes, he got the point, I will have him taste everything he cooks for you though." William answered.

I interjected, "I got a better idea William you taste everything he cooks for Crystal."

"Why is that a good idea Joseph? It's only a joke." William asked.

"You taste everything now on William. It's due to your mismanagement that the chef is out of line. I am going to sleep. I think Suki wants to share your bed tonight Joseph." Crystal said without rancor.

"Oh, Joseph it was terrible." Suki said.

I gave Suki a sour look. "You don't want to have sex but to talk."

Suki smiled like a vixen. "I am quite normal far as sex goes Joseph."

Suki came on strong but I couldn't do it. I kept seeing her as a victim. I couldn't add to it. Frustrated she smacked me on the chest and said. "Bad man, the first time we are alone, and you won't get it up."

I told her there would be other times but right now I couldn't get it out of my head that I was taking advantage of her. Grumbling she fell asleep with her head nestled in my armpit. It felt great.

A sharp whistle woke me up. Suki was in the bathroom taking a shower. Crystal stood above me. She was dressed in dungarees and a red checkered lumberjack's shirt. Soft leather gloves were stuffed in her back pocket. "Up Joseph, we have business to take care of, where is the money?"

I pointed to the closet. She took it and put it in a carpetbag and she wrote out an IOU for a million five hundred thousand. I got dressed fast as I could. Suki took her sweet time making Crystal edgy. Suki dressed in dungarees too but her checkered shirt was green. I refused to wear the dungarees and shirt they laid out for me. I wore my freshly pressed suit pants and a polo shirt I found in the closet.

The van was in the garage. The Swede was fussing with the engine like a nervous hen.

"Are you sure you don't want me to drive you?"

"No, your green card is in danger," Crystal replied emphatically, "and I thought you were leaving."

"I am mum but the plane is not leaving till eleven o'clock tonight."

I got behind the wheel and drove to Miami. It was simple, I just followed the satellite positioning device in the Van. We had an hour before the meeting was to take place. Crystal was fussing with a long box and a shopping bag full of something. She said it was long stem roses from her garden. Suki was going to give it to Hugo as a sign of peace.

The hour passed quickly. I drove up the ramp to the fourth floor ready to park the van as instructed. Crystal reminded me that we were going to meet on the top floor. I drove up to the fifth floor. There were two men standing at the end of the ramp.

Crystal jumped out of the van carrying a shotgun that she got from the long box. She stuck the gun in the older man's face. I guessed he was Hugo. The other man was a roily-poly man, an ornament, to make Hugo look tough.

Hugo's face was ashen but he was seething with anger. "You will never get away with it, I will hunt you down."

Crystal smacked him across the face with the barrel of the shotgun. Blood trickled down the sides of his mouth. Hugo's dentures went flying across the floor. He looked like an old defeated man. Suki was facing the ramp her shotgun shaking in her hands. We were expecting Hugo's reinforcement but nobody came. I thought, the arrogance of the man he didn't expect anything but obedience from Suki."

Even now Suki was afraid to look the man in the eye. I took the shotgun from Suki. She ran to the van and came back with duck tape. The fat man made it clear that he was just doing a job so he didn't put up resistance as Suki wrapped the duck tape around him. The fat man took it in stride but Hugo tried to kick her. Crystal hit him across the nose with the shotgun Hugo crumpled to the ground blood gushing from the wound.

Suki wrapped him in duck tape like a mummy. She left his crotch uncovered. She said hysterically, "lets see the biggest penis in the world," She yanked down his zipper. An ordinary penis popped out of the underwear, "is this it?" Suki laughed and wrapped his penis with duct tape. She wrapped it with so much tape that the penis was large as a horses. Hugo was coming around. We got the coke out of the trunk of their Cadillac and put in the van and we were on our way. Hugo screamed after us "I'll find and kill you son-of-bitches the hard way."

I had no doubt, if he could he would, my hands were shaking on the steering wheel.

I was driving far too fast for the tight turns of the garage. I almost flipped the van. I forced myself to calm down and drive like nothing happened. I kept thinking we should have killed him. He didn't look like a man who would stop hunting us even if we gave the coke back. What a fucking mess.

I exited the garage way to fast. As luck would have it there was a cop car with two cops searching somebody else's car. They were busy. One of the cops waived us on impatiently. I got on the highway and put the cruise control on sixty-five miles an hour and prayed that we wouldn't be stopped with a hundred kilos of coke in the car.

him. I go cross eyed when I get angry and can't aim straight. Take your money and go. Never come back again. Meanwhile I am going to hunt him through the house. I know all his hiding places. I am his wife by the way."

"I left the Yogi's place in a hurry. The last thing I heard was shots fired by the crossed eyed woman. The result made the papers the next day, a famous yogi is shot in the ass, by his jealous wife."

"The police wanted the Yogi to press charges but he refused. His wife promised to do the same thing to the woman dilly dallying with him but not before she went back to India to get an eye operation. She claimed she was aiming for his heart when she shot him in the ass. The Yogi stood next her like a wooden idol."

"When she finished with the press the Yogi limped after her like a wounded hound. She is the daughter of a very rich Maharajah. The rich Maharajah insists that in his family the custom is that a man and his wife were united for life if not daddy would get mad and cut her off from her allowance which was considerable".

"I buried my mother and had the Bugatti restored. It was her ghost you saw Suki."

Suki was properly impressed. We left the Burger King after each of us ate three Whoppers. We were hungry. I drove south toward the Keys. I kept a close eye on the mirror but nobody followed us. After driving for two hours in circles we checked into a Howard Johnson's motel. The place was not to our liking. Suki refused to stay. I found a Hilton and we stayed there for the night. We called William the next morning. He told us to come home, because Hugo was dead. A jealous sex slave got him. The male slave shot him in the head twice. It was not a good day for Hugo.

William was busy planning his future as a woman. He was being fitted for a wedding gown when we arrived. I had just one question.

"Does the groom know that he was getting married?"

"No," answered William unconcerned, "but he will darling. Right now he is on a cruise to Alaska when he returns I will pop the question. Are you satisfied Joseph?" His falsetto was coming out in baritone.

"I leased a ship Crystal, five million dollars for ten days of full royal regalia. I mean everything, darling. I even got a bunch of Buddhist monks to marry us."

Alarm bells started ringing in my head. "What kind of Buddhist monks?"

"What do you mean what kind of monks? The only kind I know is Tibetans. You know the laughing monks." William answered deflated.

"You are sure about that William? They are not Chinese by any chance?" I insisted.

William started fluttering. He told the dress fitter to get out of the room in his normal voice.

"I assumed they were Tibetans. My Formosan detectives reported that Cathy Chin was on her way to Taiwan via Hawaii skipping her California stop. Two women detectives are following her on the plane. They won't lose her. Thanks a lot Joseph that is what I needed right now is paranoia."

Crystal picked up her cell phone and said. "Give me their number William?"

He gave her a number that she dialed. When the party answered she simply asked, "Are you Chinese or Tibetans?" We could hear the loud laughter and answer on the speakerphone.

"We are Tibetans and who am I speaking to dear lady."

"The Dragon Lady," Suki laughed, I guess she could hear the guy talking on the speakerphone of her cell phone.

Suki pulled off her underwear and said, "I am taking a shower Joseph come join me," wiggling her behind at me. I got up to go with her but Crystal grabbed my arm and held me back.

"Is five million too much for three hundred people Joseph? You are an accountant you should know about these things."

I did a rough estimation in my head. "It comes to around sixteen thousand per person. Where I come from that is a lot of money but for you it might be a bargain considering it's a ten-day cruise. Will there be gambling?"

"Yes," William answered, "the shipping company runs it for fifty five percent of the profit."

"What if there is a loss who pays for that?" Crystal asked.

"The shipping company said there is never a loss it's just the question, how much of a profit, if you have a lot of high rollers the profit is large. I intend to invite a lot of rich gays. I will be their queen transvestite darlings."

"Don't you think ten days are too long?" Suki asked pulling her panties back on. It was so sexy that even got William's attention. "Most of the people will lose their money in the first couple days of the cruise."

"That is why we have helicopters darling. People will come and go. It will be fun. Will you really pick up the check Crystal?"

"I said I would William. I think the shipping company expects to make a lot of money on gambling, but I am not going on the ship. My maternal grandparents and the rest of my family got wiped out under similar circumstances."

"Don't be silly Crystal. This is a cruise ship not a yacht."

"Oh, hell William, you know I want to be there, but a lot of accidents can happen in ten days, the Bermuda Triangle and all that."

"It won't be the same without you Crystal but I will have it with or without you."

"I was hoping, you would call it off if I didn't go with you sweetie, but you were always a selfish bitch William. I'll go just to see your balls cut off."

"Oh!" I said. "I even felt that cut."

William looked around bewildered. "That is the end of my line isn't it? My man had better be worth it."

"As a doctor I advise you to take a week off and think things over William," Suki said seriously.

"I have darling, I have and I am going through with it, what a sham you are Suki. You can think after all. You are not just a cunt in heat." William replied in a sexy baritone. "Out of my room everybody that dress fitter has to size my dress today but before you go let me look at the hundred pounds of coke you just inherited from Hugo."

"It's in the safe in Joseph's new room between Suki's and my room." Crystal answered. "I wouldn't snort too much though. It's pure. You might get a heart attack."

"Ok! Ok! By the way the chef quit, he said he couldn't work in a house where there was no trust."

"Too bad the food was pretty good, I will interview a new one sweetie, I will not need a food taster after all." Crystal answered flippantly.

"Just how long are you staying in the Palace darling?" William asked in his baritone falsetto.

"Until I get bored William. Until I get bored. Hugo is off our back. Cathy Chin is on her way to Taiwan. Things haven't looked this relaxed since I met you Joseph."

I said, "lets not forget we have servants, refer to the coke now on as the new painting."

"I like the sound of "New sculpture better," Suki corrected.

That's a second good idea Suki. Keep it up woman and I'll lose all respect for you as the ultimate hedonist." William simpered in his baritone voice.

Suki looked at him raised her skirt pulled her panties down to her knees turned around and wiggled her behind at him then she said in a husky voice. "Come and get it big boy!"

William turned red in the face and hollered on the top of his lungs "I just got an erection. You bitch you seduced me. I am getting activity in a part of me that I was about to discard as useless flesh. Suki darling I never had an erection in my life. Do you have room in your life for a pig like me?"

"I might but I belong," she rearranged her skirt and walked over to Crystal and me and said, "to Joseph and Crystal."

"I inherit five hundred million bucks on the spot if we have children. You can have four hundred and fifty million of it."

"I will take all five hundred million if I have to carry a brat for nine months."

She gave Crystal and me a hug then she walked over to William, grabbed him through his pants made a few jerking motions and William keeled over her totally breathless.

"You ever have that feeling in your life William?"

William straightened up. His face was purple as a beet. In his manager's voice he said. "I never had an orgasm in my life Suki."

"I like the arty baritone voice much better William," Suki whispered loud enough for us to hear.

"Good, I like it too, it's back again Suki." William replied.

"Good I like my man hot as the sun. William do you have those Tibetan monks on your speed dial?"

"Give it to Crystal. Crystal please call and tell them we are sending a helicopter for them. We are getting married today, William, by tonight sperm will meet egg. Who is the greatest hedonist of all time William?"

"Maybe I am," he thundered in his falsetto baritone voice, "I am ready for another orgasm."

"Maybe you should save it for your wedding night," Crystal said clapping her hands and laughing like a child.

"By the way the monks are coming but it will take three hours for them to arrange everything. They are excited about the helicopter ride."

"Have as many orgasms as you want William. My men always perform," with that she rolled her hand on his crotch a couple of times. His knees buckled again but she held him up. His face turned red but he came out of it. He cupped her face and kissed it all over, "You are great Suki just great."

She untangled herself from him and came over to me and whispered, "Nine months and I will be back Joseph unless I am pregnant again, because this pig is capable of keeping a woman pregnant all her life for five hundred million dollars."

"I heard that," William said laughing, "just give me one child to make my old man happy in whatever hell he is in then you can go back to Joseph and Crystal."

Suki walked up to him and asked, "do you give me up so easily mister?"

She gave him a rough rubbing through his pants. He collapsed from the orgasm but she held him up, "can you give me up William?"

He cupped her face and said "No!" In his loud arty baritone, "but don't think you can step all over me, Suki."

"It's funny that is what I intend to do William," with a sudden move she was out of her shoes. He was supine on the floor and she gingerly danced on his stomach. She danced with and on him until we heard the sound of a helicopter landing on the roof heliport.

We ran to the elevator where four people met us. Two sleepy looking youths dressed in yellow garbs. A very demonstrative older man dressed in a dark yellow gold toga and a purple shawl that passed over his shoulder under his arm. The fourth person was a man dressed in a western suit. He was thin and very tall. The youths carried a rectangular box that they deposited on the floor with care. The older man laughing in a rich tenor voice wanted a large empty room to perform the ceremony.

Crystal led him to the music room. She had the maids roll out the piano. The older man said the wood floor was perfect but the rugs had to go. Grumbling the maids rolled up the rugs but refused to carry them out. A calm word from the tall skinny man and the two lazy youths made a big show of dragging the rugs out.

When they were done, they deposited the rectangular box, in the middle of the room. The old man had an infectious smile on his face. He laughed as he spoke. We couldn't help but laugh with him. Clapping his hands happily he said he was going to make a special mandala for long healthy life, happiness and children.

The two youths looked less enthused. One whispered word from the guy with the suit and they became active. The box was full of bottles with different colored sand in them.

The youths started creating the mandala whispering esoteric mantras as they made a circular mandala from pastel colored sand. The mandala took them two hours to finish. In the center of the mandala there was an empty space covered with crimson sandalwood. The happy monk told Suki and William to step in the center of the circle without stepping on the rest of the mandala.

The young monks lit enough incense to create a large plume of smoke in the room. Everybody got high from the smoke and started laughing without much reason. The old monk laughing recited a whole bunch of mantras. He handed the couple kerchiefs to give to each other then pronounced William and Suki man and wife.

The young man slowly erased the mandala with their feet. Suki angrily kicked at one of the boys and cried. "Hey we paid for that don't you destroy it." The laughing monk said. "If we don't destroy it the mandala won't work. Do you want deformed children?"

"Hell no!" William said jumping out of the circle. Suki was defiant. "I still think it's a waste of good art work," trampling on the mandala she walked over to William. Crystal jumped all over the mandala and started kicking the colored sand all over the place. The happy monk joined her laughing wildly.

The young monks ran to the table laden with food that the maids brought in and stuffed their faces with hot curry, vegetables, salads, bread, butter and sweet rice. The man in the suit apologized for the young monks, "This is their first meal today," With wonder on her face Suki asked, "are you that poor?" One of the youths replied sarcastically, "no, it's good discipline eating rice once a day according our superior monk. He eats all the time though," the laughing Tibetan monk cuffed the boy, "it is good discipline rascal," he joined the boys at the table.

Suki and William were feeding each other food which turned into a laughing food fight they did not notice Crystal pulling me out of the room, "we are fifth wheels here right now Joseph, lets go to India. Suki's father has a plane going there at midnight." I thought about it for a second and replied. "Sure why not?"

We did not pack a bag. We were going to buy everything we needed when we got to India. When we got on the plane to our surprise we found

Suki waiting for us. She said her lips pursed petulantly. "You left me behind. Don't you love me?"

"What happened to William?" Crystal asked with surprising concern in her voice.

"When you guys left the party was over. William looked at me and realized that he still wanted his man and I realized that I had no intention of getting married to anyone except my dumb Hip Hop Japanese boy my Grand Mother Mota Lincoln found for me. William was happy to get out of it also."

"We spoke to the Monk who laughed and annulled us happily. He told us he didn't have so much fun since he left Tibet. He refused to accept the money we offered but as they were leaving the tall man in the suit took the check out William's hand. That made the two lazy youths laugh like hyenas. William and I kissed goodbye."

"I flew the Tibetan monks to their compound then I had the helicopter deliver me to the airport. Now if you guys don't mind I will change into my Japanese schoolgirl costume to please my Dad. By the way the Tibetan Monk said a crew of Chinese nuns were asking around for a very rich Anglo woman, a Japanese woman and a guy who was in a terrible plane accident not long ago."

"Oh no!" Crystal and I groaned, "Cathy Chin found us." We got on the plane speechless but before the plane could take off the tower stopped it and a Japanese lady with big red platform sneakers got on. Looking at our glum faces Di Di said. "I presume you heard Cathy Chin is in town with William's private women investigators following her. It is definitely a good idea to go to India."

"The plane accident caused by the Heron and the brave Asian pilot's good landing was so unusual that it made the papers in Taiwan and Los Angeles, they had a photo of you getting in the limo Joseph, Cathy must have recognized you."

"We told you it was bad luck to get photographed Joseph." Crystal and Suki said in angry unison.

"Cathy Chin and the Iho Forklift fraud Joseph, I see nothing but trouble in our future." Crystal whispered under her breath as the private jet took off for the super trip to India.

It was stiflingly hot when the plane landed in India after a couple of refueling stops. Suki took charge and hired a stretch limo to take us to a five star hotel in New Delhi. We bought disposable cell phones at the airport. Suki called the hotel and reserved the Presidential suite for us.

I could see from Crystal's glum look that she was counting the money it all cost but Suki would have nothing less. "Don't look so glum Crystal my father's company will pay for it." Crystal cheered up when she found that it was not her money Suki was spending so lavishly.

Di Di couldn't pass up the opportunity to needle Crystal about being cheap. To our surprise Crystal started sobbing. "It's that little Indian Guru, he put fear into me, because he said if I didn't watch myself I would lose all my money. He hexed me. Every time I spend large sums of money his words come to me."

Di Di embraced her and told her gently. "Don't worry Crystal we are here in India we will pay the little man a visit and see if we could take the hex off you. Meanwhile start spending money maybe the fear will leave your mind."

"Yes lets do that. We will visit the Guru. He and his wife live in her father's palace in Karnataka. I'll call William he has the address. She kissed Di Di and said. "I am glad you came along Witch you brought a terrible fear to the surface of my mind. It has been bothering me since my mother's unhappy accident."

Returning to her old self she said. "Why don't you pay for the rooms Joseph? You have plenty of money now."

My heart sank to my feet. In the rush to leave Florida I forgot about the money. I left the money in the safe with the coke. I only had the fifty thousand dollars that I stuffed in my pocket before we left New York.

Di Di looked at my face and started laughing. "You left something behind didn't you Joseph? Don't worry it is in the plane with a kilo of coke, I put it in a box that is supposed to have medical matter in it."

"What about customs? Won't they find it?" I stuttered. "God we could get arrested."

"Don't worry it is in a fridge that is used for transplants they won't open it. It has a lock on it. I instructed Mr. Toyota's office to pick them up without opening it. We will pick it up when we get settled in the hotel."

"What if they open it at the office?"

"They won't Joseph but if they do they will find three packages of money and a package that is tightly wrapped in black plastic. They won't know what it is. They are from Japan, it will never occur to them that it is drugs. It's not the first time that a large sum of money was shipped from one country to another by the company. There won't be questions. After all it is the boss's daughter."

It sounded reassuring but my knees were shaking until we got into the limo in India. I started relaxing when we passed the gates of the airport.

Crystal ordered the limo driver to roll up the partition and asked Di Di why she brought the coke. Di Di responded, "because I wanted to."

Crystal tried to argue but Di Di closed her eyes and refused to answer any further question pointing to the driver who seemed to be paying a lot of attention to our conversation maybe he could read lips or something.

I was nervous all the way to the hotel. Crystal was nervous too. Suki was totally oblivious to the problem she trusted Di Di to the max again.

The hotel turned out be a Grand Hotel. The suite was on the top floor and had four bedrooms that looked over New Delhi. There was a Jacuzzi, a sauna and a little gym and smelly flowers everywhere. There was a butler and maids at the ring of a bell. It was true luxury.

We did not have a change of clothes but that was no problem. There was a tailor on the premises who prepared freshly tailored clothing within twenty four hours. I ordered some slacks, shirts and jackets. Silk underwear and socks were ready made from China but they were top quality that you never saw in the USA.

The women were fitted by a seamstress who made the latest styles by copying pictures from Vogue. We spent fifty thousand dollars on clothing. I felt like fricking prince. Even Crystal was impressed.

We lounged around the hotel for a week letting our bodies get used to the searing heat. Di Di had a grand old time ordering the servants around. She was really hard on a beautiful tall skinny maid named Indira who seemed oblivious to her criticism.

We made a habit of eating breakfast on the balcony overlooking the bustling city. To my surprise Indira who served us the food was wearing a garish red bra like thing decorated with quarter size mirrors, colored sequins and red pantaloons decorated with the same motif as the bra. The mark between her eyes normally red was gold and she had a large ruby gem in her bellybutton.

Di Di eyed her with a mean look in her eyes. Man, I thought, Indira is going to get it.

To my surprise Indira was gracious. She dismissed the four waiters who brought up the food and served me first then Crystal, Suki then Di Di who was dressed in a black day kimono decorated with small white flowers instead of red tennis shoes she had Japanese wooden clogs on her feet.

Indira handed Di Di a glass of mango lassi a yogurt drink. Di Di put it to her lips without taking her eyes of Indira who stopped smiling. Indira said with mirth in her voice, "it is Kali's birthday in Rajastan where I come from."

Di Di replied. "Big deal darling, it is always someone's birthday somewhere in the world," and took a deep drink of the lassi.

Di Di gave out a holler and spit the drink in my lap. The lassi was full of glass shards size of silver dollars blood was dribbling down her chin.

She jumped up knocking the table over and at the same time she pulled out her hairpins. Her long black hair cascaded down her back and face. She looked like a Kabuki ghost dancer.

Indira produced a weird looking scissor and the two women started fighting. Di Di's hairpins were deadly she killed the sushi boy with them in Florida.

Indira's scissor looked wicked too big enough to cut flesh to ribbons it was a fight to the death.

Di Di struck first by stabbing Indira in the shoulder but Indira was fast as cobra she jumped back before the pin could go in more than two inches. The fighting was fast and furious both women were a bloody mess in minutes.

Meanwhile, Suki started wailing something in Japanese and Crystal joined her singing in a language I never heard before. The noise and the battle was immensely exciting, it was Kali's birthday in Rajastan.

Somehow both women lost their weapons. They started hand to hand combat pulling each other's hair and grappling like marionettes, as if a mad puppeteer, was pulling the strings.

They fell on the floor rolling back and forth. Di Di was on top she pinned both of Indira's arms to the floor. Indira stopped fighting her she just lay there limp. Their eyes met Di Di kissed Indira on the mouth lustily, Indira responded by grinding her belly against Di Dis. The women made love feverously.

I never saw anything like it. I was fascinated and disgusted at the same time. Suki and Crystal must have felt the same way, because both of them threw up, it was Kali's birthday in Rajastan.

After a couple of minutes the women got up and ran to the Jacuzzi all we heard was laughing and giggling.

Crystal pulled herself together and rang for the butler whose face was ashen. He ordered the servants to clean up the place.

He pulled me aside and said. "Be careful sir it is a Tantric night wild women are looking for kings to send to moksha. Liberation from the cycle of death through sex, they sometimes ride a man to Nirvana if you know what I mean sir?

"I don't know what you mean but I know it is Kali's birthday in Rajastan." He put two fingers on my lips and said. "Don't say her holy name she might hear you and take your skull if you know what I mean sir?"

"No! I don't but I get the general idea, it is Kali's birthday in Rajastan."

"Yes, sir, a night of sin for a Tantrika. Those who do not eat flesh will eat meat those who don't drink alcohol will drink wine and who never harm anybody will kill, it is Kali's mad sexual dance to reach Samadhi the highest form of meditation."

I was so mesmerized by his words I did not notice he was reaching for a hidden dagger in his belt but he was stopped by Indira's commanding voice. "Rajiv we ride to Nirvana now."

She was naked her breast's covered by her raven black hair bloody spots all over her body. She held a tray which had a jeweled crown, bottle of rice wine, meat cakes and a tiny bottle of something with a mercury compound in it and a cake of red sandalwood paste with red mercury mixed in it.

Rajiv shrunk visibly and whined. "Why me Mother? Why today?"

"Are you backing out Rajiv?" Indira asked dejected.

"Hell no baby, I am ready if you are, it was only the pacifist vegetarian in me, trying to escape. This is the day I have been waiting for ten years, baby, to unite with Mother Kali, I am a Tantrika forever. Bless my Guru's lotus feet."

Rajiv took the crown and put it on his head and told us to sit cross legged in a semi-circle, in a commanding voice. We sat down. just then Di Di came in naked, holding Brown's shiny gun with the silencer on it, and sat with us in the semi-circle.

"Where the hell did the gun come from Di Di?" Crystal wanted to know.

"The transplant cases they were delivered last night. The money is all there Joseph."

"If you guys can stop chattering we can start the ceremony." Rajiv said sarcastically.

We shut up and watched Rajiv get undressed. He had a big penis.

A door opened on a wall where there was no door before and a very old man came through it. He was dressed in a crimson robe. He had long hair he reminded me of Maharishi Yogi. Purity emanated from him.

Rajiv bowed deeply before him and kissed the feet of his Guru. Indira looked at the Guru with contempt and gave him the finger that only seemed to energize the Guru.

Rajiv at the Gurus instruction took the red sandalwood paste with red mercury in it and applied it on the sole of Indira's feet. He applied a generous amount between her eyebrows. Indira became cross eyed and her body took on a golden hue. She swayed in ecstasy. The Guru told her firmly to sit still, she tried to obey but she could not.

The Guru showed Rajiv hand motions which he called yoni mudras, then he told Rajiv to drink the content of the little bottle that would take effect, after he and Indira ate the meat cakes and drank the wine. Revulsion came on Rajiv's face when he ate the meat and drank the wine. The Guru whispered mantras with each action. Indira seemed to be in ecstasy in a different world.

Rajiv's movements seemed labored and he took on a cyanotic blue color and his penis became big and hard. The Guru told him to touch different parts of her body with his thumb reciting a mantra with each touch he called it Nyasa.

The Guru told Rajiv to put a dab of the sandalwood between our eyebrows, in no time I was in seventh heaven, Di Di, Crystal and Suki looked like they were there too. I felt a movement of energy at the base of my spine.

The Guru told Rajiv to lie on the floor on his back. In a detached way I found Rajiv amusing lying there with his big blue penis sticking up in the air.

The Guru took a mirror and stuck it under Rajiv's nose there was no vapor coming out of his nose or mouth, the Guru whispered, "Rajiv's prana is in his lingam O' Holy reincarnation of Mother Kali you can unite with him now."

The Guru gathered himself together and walked through the door. Two women came through the wall carrying swords. One was jet black the other white as old ivory. The ivory colored woman stood at Rajiv's head and the jet black woman stood at Rajiv's foot. They stood on one leg while their left leg crossed over their thigh.

Indira mounted Rajiv and rode him for what seemed like hours, we watched them, totally detached on some other plane, in utter bliss.

Indira screamed as she shook with a humongous orgasm, Maayaii Kali we are one. Rajiv ejaculated the dead man came, life transcends death."

The Jet black woman cut off Indira's head while she was in the height of her orgasm. To my horror headless Indira picked up her own decapitated head and continued riding Rajiv. She had a beautiful smile on her face and her eyes rested on us without fear.

The horror and the bliss I was experiencing pushed the snake like energy up my spine. It reached the Thousand Petal Lotus above my head. I saw Shiva and Kali in the ten thousand year embrace. I became a god I became one with the stars and galaxies that were swirling around me.

I saw headless Indira ride dead Rajiv for a long time, I thought I understood Tantra.

After a while I became sleepy and went to bed so did the women leaving the still coupling pair behind.

When I woke up it was in the middle of the night. I went to the living room where there was no sign of the epic struggle that took place during the day.

Instead there was a table laden with food all vegetarian. I drank some mango juice and saw myself in a mirror there was a red mark between my eyes so it wasn't a dream after all.

Suki joined me. There was a red mark on her brow too. "I had this incredible dream Joseph I became a goddess after watching this incredible sex scene between Rajiv and Indira." Suki said with wonder in her voice.

"It wasn't a dream Suki I became a goddess too." Di Di said coming over to the table and grabbing a shiny red apple.

Her body was covered with fresh cuts her sagging breast showed her age. Crystal came in naked rubbing her eyes. "I think I went crazy last night. I keep thinking I am some sort of goddess. Am I? We walked around naked without shame.

I said with wonder. "I think so I had the same dream. That scene between Rajiv and Indira must have blown my mind. I think I am god too."

"So we have become gods we shall see." Suki chirped scratching her pubic hair. "Lets call the staff."

Looking at her I got an erection. Crystal came over and kissed my penis and laughed. "Bless you, Shiva lingam, the giver of the seed of life." Suki did the same thing but Di Di just touched it and put her hand on her lips repeating the mantra.

We all jumped in the Jacuzzi. Sitting in the hot swirling water the memory of the horror and ecstasy came over me. I felt something moving at the base of my spine and suddenly I felt something like a snake ascending up around my spine area. I felt fear.

Rajiv's Guru appeared floating in the air as if on a television screen; he said in a heavenly voice. "Don't try to block the movement of the Kundalini, because it could drive you insane if the energy goes through the wrong channels."

My fear went away and incredible bliss took over as the snake like force went through my Chakras climbing trough my body to an inch above my head to the Thousand Petal Lotus. I was in pure ecstasy.

I heard millions of chirping sounds. "What is that sound?" The women and I asked together.

We were sitting cross legged in the lotus position in a semi-circle around the Guru in the Thousand Petal Lotus blossom. He said in a soft voice. "That is the sound of millions of fish talking; in this lotus you can hear the fish talk to each other."

Di Di bowed before the Guru and asked him to make love to her. He laughed. "I had my children. I am no longer in the householder stage. I am celibate except on Kali's birthday which passed at midnight. But you four can."

Suddenly I was facing three giant female spiders they were beckoning to me with lust. I a male spider was tiny compared to them. The urge to unite with them overwhelmed me. Without fear even though they might eat me I climbed on each gorgeous monster and deposited my sperm sack. The female spiders and I were in heavenly happiness.

Before long we were back in a semi circle around the Guru who was beaming. "I was going to eat you Joseph." Crystal laughed but you were so tiny and cute I had to let you have your way with me.

I puffed up my chest and said. "So this is Tantra?"

"Yes in the Thousand Petal Lotus blossom. Now your Kundalini, the energy you felt moving at the base of your spine will descend and you will be back in the Jacuzzi. Time has come for you to visit ancient India there are thousands of temples for tourist to visit. If you find something puzzling just think of me and I will come to you."

"Dear Guru." I asked. "Why did Rajiv and Indira eat the meat cakes?"

"Rajiv was a very religious Hindu. Eating meat especially cow meat was a terrible shock to his system it awoke his Kundalini; the serpent like thing you all felt moving at the base of your spine. It takes many years of meditation to awaken the Kundalini. Shock with the help of mercury compounds will force the Kundalini upwards through the energy centers of the body to the Thousand Petal Lotus where Shiva and his Shakti unite as it happened to you."

"The little bottle Rajiv and Indira drank contained a mercury compound that forced their Kundalini into the second energy center, the sexual center; the rest of their body and energy centers died.

"A god and goddess rule each energy center called Chakras. With the help of these deities the transitional body can perform wonderful things like the beheading of Indira; she actually watched herself become a demigoddess through her decapitated head.

"The whole point of Tantra is to get a glimpse of the sphere where the god's live and get their favor."

"Indira was an ordinary woman she was a just vehicle for Rajiv to get a glimpse of the Thousand Petal Lotus, he had no ambition of becoming a god he certainly didn't want die. He was a total pacifist just like the Jain. Killing a human being was totally abhorrent to him."

I interrupted. "Let me guess he was going to kill somebody hoping to shock his Kundalini in to action."

"Yes, you four were going to be his victims," the Guru smiled, "his friend the limo driver overheard Di Di mention that you smuggled cocaine into the country. The killings would have been dismissed as drug deal gone sour."

"Di Di saved your lives. Indira was shocked and shamed when she responded sexually to Di Di's kiss."

"Her Kundalini which was never active ripped through the first Chakra and got stuck in her second Chakra; the sex Chakra. The gods Vishnu and Rakini controlling the Chakra must have taken charge, because those two women with the swords came out of nowhere. I did not send them."

"You saw Rajiv tried to back out when Indira called out to him but it was too late Indira was in charge."

"In Hindustan people pay a lot of lip service to the power of Shakti (female) energy but for the first time in my sixty years of practicing Tantra; I saw its power I am humbled and blessed by Mother Kali to have witnessed it in its full force."

"Children, I fear for my life, because for sixty years I have been a sham. I have many disciples; ninety-nine percent men. Tantric yoga requires couples so I hire whores for my disciples to practice with. Most of the whores think it's easy money and enjoy being around religious men who treat them as goddesses as long as we paid them money."

"Every once in a while a whore becomes a disciple but it doesn't last long, because the tricks they learn doing Tantra makes them valuable in the street. Pimps steal them from me."

"Indira was different, she came from Rajiv's village in Rajastan, a religious girl who respected me as her Guru. She was chaste but every once in a while she gave into Rajiv's advances hoping to marry him, tonight was supposed to be one of those nights.

"Rajiv told me that he was going to kill you guys tonight. I went along knowing that I would stop him but things got out hand. The fight between Di Di and Indira was totally unexpected."

"In my sixty years as a Guru and student I never saw Shakti power like it; and when those two women with the swords arrived from nowhere I feared for my life. They gave me the little bottle and the red sandalwood paste."

"I decided to perform the ceremony exactly as the ancient text instructed. The text was from the eighteen century Rajastan a very active period for Tantra in Hindustan."

"You lying shit! You are a bunch of thugs who were going to kill and rob us. That is why you used that secret door." Suki screeched. I tried to focus on her face but there was a black aura about her truly frightening.

"No, Mother please I had no such intentions. That door leads to the old servant quarters; it was walled off when the hotel was renovated. Rajiv discovered it accidentally a couple of years ago."

"This suite is seldom rented, because it's very expensive so I started using it for my Tantra meetings. The management does not mind. The managing agent's son is a disciple of mine a total imbecile, but he pays for the whores."

Suki stuck her tongue out at him; it was blood red but she stopped using the scary voice. The Guru was visible frightened. In a shaky voice he asked; Mother Kali am I forgiven?

Suki cross eyed told him. "Maybe, but no more lies." Turning to Di Di she asked. "What was between you and Indira?"

"Hate, love, who the hell knows, I think I was doing my routine guarding you Suki." Di Di replied bored. I think my protecting you is coming to an end too Suki. I have to get back to my husband I need his Jewish intellect to get me out of this mess, Guru do you have any more of that red paste?

"Yes. The coal black woman gave me a large tub of it."

"I'll take some of it and try it on him. After all these years with me he could handle anything, perhaps we could screw ourselves to Nirvana. I am leaving when the sun comes up. I will see you in Tokyo next year Suki. I am tired, I am going to bed. Bring me the red paste before I leave Guru."

"Thanks for saving us Milk Mother. I'll see you in Tokyo at the next meeting of the Demented Clown Society, we will blow the Ancient's mind."

Turning to the Guru, Suki asked. "Do you need money?"

"Yes Mum, I am going to use only high class courtesans for my disciples, very expensive."

"Don't worry about it Suki; I will build him an ashram in Rajastan." Crystal offered excitedly.

I looked at Crystal, her aura was pure as white gold.

"So it is all set. Don't forget the paste Guru!" Di Di said as she walked to her bedroom with pride in her step.

"How did you get in the Thousand Petal Lotus with us Guru?" I asked.

"For sixty years I thought I could move my Kundalini up and down but it was an illusion I moved nothing. When those two women appeared they threatened to cut my head off. To emphasize the fact the ivory colored women cut the skin on my left wrist and put a drop of the red paste on my forehead. She told me I better not slip up with the ceremony."

"At the sight of the blood I felt movement between my lingam and anus; my Kundalini awoke. I let it ascend through my Chakras until I reached the crowning glory the Sahasrara the Thousand Petal Lotus. When you four joined me there; I was truly pleased."

"I think the whole thing was mass hypnosis just like the Indian rope trick." Crystal said laughing.

"I am afraid not Miss if you read the papers tomorrow morning the police will report that Rajiv and headless Indira and her decapitated head were found in a ditch not far away from the hotel. They will blame it on Rajiv who in a jealous rage killed Indira then committed suicide."

"How come you are not a god Guru?"

"It's my Karma; for sixty years I have been lying to the gods about me and my disciples abilities now that it happened for real the gods; will not accept me. I have to perform many austerities before they welcome me as a demigod."

"Will you really build me an ashram, Miss?"

"Sure, how much do you need?" Crystal answered without her usual hesitation about spending money.

"A three thousand a month will rent a nice villa on the outskirts of Delhi. I hope it is not too much."

You misunderstand me Guru I said I will build you an ashram in Rajastan not here in New Delhi."

"Miss I am a cosmopolitan man. I can't live in Rajastan it would be a prison."

"I didn't say you have to live there all the time but all your Tantric activities will take place in Rajastan. From what I heard today Rajastan is center of the cult they will understand you there, you won't be able to pull trick like you pulled on us beloved. The police will know if you do it again, that it is cult activity not a suicide and take appropriate action."

"How does a million and a half dollars for the building of the ashram and five hundred thousand for upkeep for the next twenty years sound? You should be able to hire plenty of courtesans for your disciples with that much cash."

"Mum Sahib, I am speechless. Of course I will do it in Rajastan you have been reincarnated as Lakshmi the golden Goddess, let me worship at your lotus feet."

"You can worship me, I will give you a check for two million dollars which should take care of the building the ashram and the first years upkeep, but if you double cross me you will be lucky to have no luck at all. Is there a City Bank in New Delhi?"

"Yes there is Miss."

"She got up to get her check book her ass looked really great. I got aroused. Without looking back she said "It will be fun to do it in the morning Joseph. What is your name Guru?"

"Piri, Prakash Piri Miss. I live in a little room here in the hotel in exchange for teaching the manager's foolish son Tantra."

Crystal came back dressed in a pink silk nightgown. "Here is your check and my card. Call the number when the ashram is ready for the dedication."

I looked at Suki but she was sleeping in the sitting position cradling the gun she seemed totally relaxed for a change.

"Before you go Guru Piri let us have the tub of red paste and the rest of the liquid stuff you put in the little bottle." I asked.

"Ok Sir, but the stuff in the bottle is very dangerous. Its use is outlawed here in India so be careful when you go through customs."

He got up from the lotus position and walked through the secret door, he backed back into the room with his hands up in the air.

A tall Chinese woman dressed in yellow nun's robe came through the door holding a gun followed by two Asian women crying and a boy of sixteen, ashen faced. Cathy Chin found us.

"Finally I got you son-of-bitches goodbye this is for my poor sweet brother."

But before she could shoot she developed a large red third eye and dropped to the floor dead. The two women started shouting. "Don't shoot we are the detectives you hired to follow her around. She caught us, look, look she put explosive belts on us, we had to follow her orders."

The women raised their yellow nun's gowns and sure enough they were wearing gun belts with batteries attached to them,

I asked. "When did you arrive?" They replied in unison; "yesterday."

I walked up to them and yanked the batteries off the belt. One of them passed out the other one defecated. Her odor filled the room.

I opened the cartridge cases on the gun belt. They held children's plastic clay.

Suki walked over to me holding Brown's shiny smoking gun with the silencer on the boy.

The Guru jumped front of the boy. "Don't shoot, he is the manager's son. He was guarding the downstairs door.

"Some guard." Suki laughed. Her laughter broke the tension. The Chinese woman detective, who defecated, apologized profusely.

Crystal took her by the hand and led her to the bathroom.

I said. "Thank God Di Di threw the gun in Suki's lap when she went to bed."

Crystal came back with a glass of water for the other woman detective. "You are very brave Joseph." She patted my lingam. I kept forgetting I was naked.

"I knew there was no danger. There was no way she could get explosives through customs these days, no matter how smart she is."

"Where did she get the gun?" Suki wanted to know.

The woman detective answered sheepishly. "I have a special permit to carry firearms on a plane. She must have seen it in my pocketbook, on the plane."

"How did she get it from you?" Suki insisted.

"Somebody let her into our room. She punched me in the mouth and grabbed my pocketbook."

"Where did she get the gun belt and the clay?"

The boy turned red. The Guru jumped on the boy. What happened; Nandi? Tell me the truth."

"I was at the desk when she arrived. I couldn't keep my eyes off her. I never saw such a beautiful woman even though she had a shaved head. She must have noticed, because she pulled me aside and told me if I did her a favor she would kiss me."

"She showed me a newspaper with Mr. Goodwin's picture. She wanted a plastic key to get in to your room. I told her about the hidden, servant's quarters. She asked me to get the gun belts and plastic clay and batteries. I led her up here. You are not going to tell the police are you Guru?"

"No you can leave but don't tell anybody not a sound to anybody you stupid boy."

"The Guru dialed a number on his cell phone and told somebody to come and pick up a package. He told us to strip Cathy Chin of her robe. His men would not touch a Nun. Half hour later two husky men showed up and took naked Cathy Chin to hell, I hope.

The two Chinese women detectives pulled themselves together and left. They said they would send a report to William.

"The Guru kissed us all and left whispering that it was very bad karma to kill a priestess. I told him Cathy Chin was not a Buddhist nun but a very bad gangster. He cheered up considerably and promised to call Crystal when the ashram was built.

"We are going to Japan tomorrow Suki and take care of Mr. Iho of Iho Forklift Company, now let's go to bed."

I went to my bedroom. I fell asleep before my head hit the pillow.

Next morning I found a pound tub of the red paste and a pint bottle of the other compound on the side table with an attached note saying if I wanted to stop people from coming and going through the door push the sofa against the wall.

I went to Di Di's bedroom to give her some of the red paste but she was gone. There was a note on the bed. It said the Guru came by and gave her some of the red paste and his blessing. She would see us in the States. Love and Kisses.

Suki said there was a Toyota Industries plane going to Japan in a couple of days. She had to bump eight unhappy executives to make room for us on the plane, she wanted us to be alone on the plane.

We spent the next couple of days touring Temples. It was strange wherever we went a priest would meet us and take us on a private tour of the Temple.

We rented a helicopter and went to see the Yogi who cursed Crystal's mother. He was very handsome in his Nehru suit. He wine and dined us and prepared a special potion to take the curse off Crystal.

His cross eyed wife was not so nice but she relented when Crystal gave her a million dollar Arabian stallion colt, it had fabulous bloodline.

Not to be outdone her father, the Maharaja, gave Crystal a jeweled crown that his mother wore on the day of India's Independence. Crystal accepted it but she left it with the Maharaja to be exhibited under Crystal's name, the Maharaja was visibly relieved to have the crown in his possession.

Finally, the day arrived for our flight. The transplant cases with the money and the cocaine were loaded on to the plane and we were on our way. The plane ride to Japan was uneventful. We slept most of the time. Suki was more assertive now; she insisted that the stewardess's stay in the back of the plane out of earshot.

Slowly the feeling that I was superhuman left me. Crystal insisted that what we saw was mass hypnosis just like the Indian rope trick.

"What is the Indian rope trick?" I asked her, I never heard of it before.

"The rope trick was first performed in the fourteenth century in South India. The Fakir throws a stout rope with a wood ball at the end of it up in to the sky, the rope does not fall back down. The Fakir's helper, a six year old boy, is ordered to climb up to find out what is up there. The boy climbs up the rope and disappears."

"The Fakir orders the boy to climb down but there is no answer. The Fakir angry, because the boy does not obey him buckles on a sword and climbs up after the boy and disappears. After a while body parts start falling out of the sky arms, legs, the torso and finally the boys head land on the ground."

"The Fakir climbs down the rope and places the boy's body parts to its appropriate positions on the torso and says a mantra and the boy jumps up and laughs at the horrified crowd."

"The European's who have seen the trick could not debunk it so they blamed it on mass hypnosis. That is what happened to us."

"You are trying to rationalize something out of the ordinary to keep your sanity Crystal. I believe what we saw was real they did find Rajiv and Indira dead near the hotel. What do you think Joseph?" Suki retorted excitedly.

"It happened as we saw and experienced it. That trip to the Thousand Petal Lotus was real too we are Tantrikas and Prakash Piri is our Guru not, because I like him but, because he studied this shit for sixty years. We need a guide and he is not so bad. I am looking forward to seeing him again. I want to visit the other Chakras in my body. I still feel the Kundalini energy moving in that spot between my penis and anus every once in a while. I am not sure what to do about it."

"I feel movement between my vagina and anus also." Replied Crystal not a bit worried, "I don't think it is a good idea to block its movement upwards, Piri said it could drive you insane if it goes through the wrong channels."

Suki whispered with tears in her eyes.

"I prefer if we didn't talk about this thing until we are alone, it is supposed to be secret. I read somewhere that the Buddhist's believe in Tantra too, but to them it is the male energy that is the moving force of the universe not the female energy. I feel more comfortable with that concept. I am going to find a Japanese Buddhist monk who can explain how to control the forces energized in my body by that stupid Guru. He told me that Kali's energy was the strongest in me.

He is afraid of me, I don't like it. The only good thing that happened is that Di Di and I changed relationships, I am no longer bound to her. I have to look out for myself that is a good thing. I know mom is going to be happy, she told me on my last birthday that it was about time I grew up, well I have thanks to that bastard Guru."

I told Suki. "It's a funny thing Suki but I feel perfectly comfortable with the female, Shakti, force being the controlling force of my universe."

Crystal concurred. "I like the idea that the Shakti force is the ultimate energy of the universe."

Suki said. "It is easy enough for you two, because your karma is not tied to Goddess Kali. I feel sorry for Cathy Chin, because she didn't have a chance. I feel sorry for myself, because I feel absolutely no remorse for killing her, a very bad thing if you are brought up as a Japanese Buddhist."

"Joseph, Piri told me that your Karma was tied to Ganesh, businessman will seek your advice and favor from all over the world and Crystal your karma is tied to Lakshmi the Goddess of good luck, wealth and all good things in the universe, the hell with you two."

"After we take care of this business with Iho Forklift I will go to America and marry the Japanese American junky boyfriend Grandma Mota Lincoln found for me. It's too bad, because I love you both madly I think Piri made a mistake with you Joseph to me you are Shiva the Destroyer, my heavenly lover."

All three of us started sobbing. We fell asleep holding hands.

The stewardess woke us up. She asked for the keys to the transplant boxes. My heart started beating a thousand beats a minute. Suki said no but the woman insisted. She said the Japanese government checked all transport boxes now, because there was a scandal about transplant trafficking.

Suki was in control of herself but Crystal and I turned white with fear. Suki refused and told the woman she would bring our boxes through customs.

The stewardess was very polite but went to the Captain who asked Suki to come to the cockpit. Suki came back smiling and gave the keys to the stewardess.

When the woman went back to her post Suki asked me if I had the twenty five thousand dollars. I told her I still had the fifty thousand in my carryon luggage. Suki was happy as a schoolgirl on her first date. I grumbled about the money but I was willing to give it to her. Suki told me I would have to give it to the pilot myself.

Suki told us that Di Di arranged with the pilot to smuggle my three million dollars and the cocaine into the country. The pilot thought he was smuggling in precious Indian art.

Di Di promised him twenty five thousand dollars for the job. We all relaxed a bit but I promised myself I would dump cocaine the first chance I had. I kicked myself forgetting to do it in India it was nothing but trouble.

I thanked heaven for Di Di's foresight but cursed her for bringing the cocaine in the first place.

When the plane landed we were met by one of Suki's employees. He bowed a half a dozen times and ushered us to through customs. An agent searched my luggage and found the fifty thousand dollars; the inspector asked me why I brought in so much money in cash. I told him it was spending money. He let me through after I signed a form indicating I brought in a large sum of money. Out of the corner of my eyes I saw a uniformed man video taping me.

As we agreed I met the pilot in the bathroom. I went into a stall and counted out twenty five thousand dollars. He was in the next stall to me. I slipped him the money under the partition. He pushed his carryon case under the partition to me, he left without saying goodbye.

When I went out of the bathroom I saw a uniformed man video taping me. I heard Suki's voice in my mind saying. "Don't worry Joseph, they are videotaping everybody."

I saw Suki and Crystal waiting for me. They were about fifty feet away, Suki was looking at me with great concentration. I hoped that Suki's employee didn't notice that I was walking out of the bathroom with an extra suitcase.

Suki came over to me and whispered. "Did you hear me? Surprised I said. "Yes." She said. "There is more to this Tantra thing then we know Joseph."

A stretch limo was waiting for us. The driver opened the door bowing a thousand times. I shook his hand, that threw him but I could see on his face that he liked it.

Crystal told the driver to take us to her apartment in the theater district of Tokyo. "I hope I catch Lila using the apartment and have the pleasure of throwing her out. The Ancient came through for me. I got a court order confirming the validity of the contract your father and I signed. I have the lease."

"Don't be so hard on mother Crystal it is impossible to get an apartment in this section of Tokyo. Every time she finds a place my father sabotages it. She hates hotels so she still uses your apartment for her trysts. From what I hear her new Kabuki player is quite ugly but a great lover I am dying to meet him. Mom and the Ancient had a big argument because he sold out to you, he won the argument but she swore to get even with him but, she doesn't know how. The Ancient doesn't care."

The apartment was on the top of a theater. It took up the whole second floor. There were ten bedrooms divided by bamboo screens that could be moved to create one large room. All the furniture was on the floor level. There was a large bed in one of the rooms with mirrors on the ceiling it must have been Lila's room. There was dust on everything. Suki ran her finger through the dust and said. "No one used this bedroom in ages. Mom must have found another place."

I went to the kitchen and looked in the fridge there was fresh food in it. "Someone is using this place. The vegetables are quite fresh." As I said it I heard a key turn in the lock of the front door.

A very old man and a young man walked through the door. I didn't have to be told it was the Ancient. He was dressed in western style suit two sizes too big. He must have been a heavier man at one time. The young man with him was dressed like Elvis in motorcycle drag.

The old man's bird like face held two eyes that were like black beads. He took in the situation calmly and said, "I live here now. You never come here Crystal. It is a shame to waste such a valuable space."

The young man pulled a switchblade knife with flourish and combed his hair with the comb that was in the place of the blade.

Crystal said. "Money-money-everybody wants money. You are not going to live here anymore old man, we are moving in."

She took out her checkbook and made out a check for twenty thousand dollars and told him to go back to his old apartment.

The old man took the check whistled and bowed his head slightly. He turned to me and said in English. "I don't know you young man but I know Crystal and Suki they have changed. You three have the aura of the Gods about you be careful where there are Gods there are Demons who want to destroy you out of vanity."

He went to the bathroom and collected his shaving kit. Young Elvis struck a pose and said in broken English don't worry. He likes to scare people. You look groovy to me." He pinched Suki's thigh.

I felt Suki's anger rising in my mind. She was reaching for her purse I thought in my mind. "Don't do it Suki he is just a kid he likes you." She looked at me and calmed down.

"A clear sharp voice spoke in my mind so you three are no longer just animals. It has been a long time since I had a mental chat."

The Ancient turned to the boy and told him to go to a bar and wait for him there. "Ok," the boy said. "But remember the clock is running."

Looking at the check the old man said, "I can afford you and your brother now."

"I am looking forward to it, if you bring the Japanese bitch along, she is hot."

Suki threw me a mental image of the boy standing on a chair with a noose around his neck. Suki walked up to the boy and kicked the chair away. The boy hung there with his tongue sticking out and his eyes bulging out of its sockets. It was like watching television but it was all happening in my mind.

"Stop it Suki!" The mental voice was clearly Crystals. *"I think he is cute."*

"You would get attracted to a male prostitute Crystal." Suki replied mentally and started laughing out loud.

The boy said. "Why are you laughing at me bitch? He flicked his switchblade and combed his hair again. Striking an Elves' pose he turned around and walked out through the front door.

He said in broken English. "I'll be seeing you all later, amigos." And he slammed the door behind him with force.

The old man said through his mouth. "So you three speak mentally. I wouldn't do it very often, because it takes up a lot of space in the brain at the expense of other functions of the brain. Didn't your teacher tell you this?

"We don't really have a teacher. Our Guru tried to kill us but somehow we came out on top. We are building an Ashram for him in India."

'Is he a demon?" The Ancient asked.

"I don't think so. It was Kali's birthday in Rajastan. He was going to sacrifice us but Di Di Sugaro turned the table on him somehow. She dumped me in India and went back to her husband in New York." Suki said grudgingly.

"I know. Your mother told me. Di Di called her from New York. Lila is looking forward to seeing you. Di Di also told Lila that your father and Mr. Iho ripped off Crystal. Lila told me about it, she tells me everything. Life is funny, the money you gave me to get you this apartment for you, went for a five inch Buddha made of medium grade jade. It is called the Buddha of the Open Mind.

"There were thirty one Buddha's made by a mediocre craftsman. One for each student of the Open Mind class for mentally gifted students, our teacher was a Shinto Monk who taught us how to fight with our minds for the government."

"He called us demi gods the direct servants of the Emperor who was the Sun God. Thirty one students started the class, ten of us survived the class, and could talk mentally to the monk and to each other. I was the only student of noble blood. Twenty one students died trying to learn mental talk. You see it is no problem starting mental talk there are drugs that start it but stopping the talk is the problem."

It is seductive, thirty one of us sat around in total silence not moving just talking mentally. Our maids considered us madmen, because the only thing we would do out loud was to laugh. This went on for a year. Our monk tried to teach us all sorts of Yoga and meditation to control our mental chatter but nothing worked."

"One day a military officer showed up and told the Shinto monk he was going to teach us to shut up when ordered. At first we thought he could hear but when we discovered he could not hear mentally we started making fun of him."

"The Shinto monk who could hear us told him what was happening. The officer pulled out his gun and shot twenty one students to death before we learned to silence our mental voice. I lost control and started shouting mentally. The Shinto monk pointed to me, the officer pointed his gun at me, to shoot me. I got so scared that I grabbed for his gun mentally and broke his arm in two places. The officer came over to me and kissed me on the forehead and left never to return."

"The next day a new Shinto monk appeared. He told us our old teacher committed suicide. The new teacher made believe that he could hear but we soon discovered that he could not and started talking mentally. The little son-of-a-bitch, he couldn't have been more than four foot eight inches tall, was very observant and would beat us with a bamboo cane if we stopped talking out loud and talked mentally."

"I am of noble blood. I have the right to see the Emperor, but his bodyguards would not let me close to him, they feared I might try to harm him from a distance. To tell the truth I tried hurting people from a distance it never worked again. I was probably so scared of dying that I performed a super human feat on that military officer. The only thing I can do mentally is to chatter."

"The little Shinto monk collected all our Buddha's and smashed them to smithereens. One of our men managed to save one. It is that jade that I bought from his widow when he died of old age. I had a little shrine built for it in a faraway Buddhist temple."

"The little monk was a true pacifist that is why he hated us, because he knew we would be used by the Militarist, he did his best to destroy the program."

"Were you used?" Suki asked with wonder in her voice. We were sitting on a bamboo mat. Crystal found some Sake in the fridge and served it to us.

"Sure they used us in the Navy. Eight guys were assigned to aircraft carriers and battle ships. I stayed behind in Tokyo my parents wouldn't hear of me leaving the land of Japan; heaven. I was the center. I would communicate with our guys when the weather was too bad for radio. Only two guys survived the war the guy with the jade Buddha and me."

"The guy with the jade Buddha was saved by the little monk. I suspect he used to signal the little monk when we talked mentally. He married the little monk's sister. The little monk reported him as mentally disabled and kept him out of the military."

"We were thought theory of mental communication. The monks thought there was an organ in the mind that could communicate but it was like an octopus. After a while if you used it often it would start reaching into other parts of the brain hindering the minds proper function. It was probably useful for ancient hunters but today it is like the appendix not very useful. And when the octopus reaches into the brain where the subconscious is stored then the telepath becomes useless, because he can no longer tell the difference between the outside voice from someone else and his own inner voice."

"What about the Kundalini?" Crystal asked gently.

"You know about that? Well if you experienced that then you are on a higher plane than I am. I am just a human radio I was born that way.

"You lying old bastard. You know all about the power of Tantra." Suki whispered.

"Perhaps I heard a few things here and there but nothing worth mentioning. We Japanese have a cognitive model of the world that all Japanese agree on. Tantra throws that model out of kilter a very dangerous thing in a homogeneous society like ours."

"You can stay with us if you want Ancient san." Crystal offered.

"Thank you but there is an old woman who waits for me to come home. I only use this place for rendezvous and meetings of the Demented Clown Society's inner circle.

"Kindness for a kindness Crystal go home there is danger for you in Japan."

"I can't. Iho Forklift is worth five billion dollars and I own it all. Mr. Iho is just a front man. Mr. Iho and Mr. Toyota are up to something and I am going to find out what."

I watched the old man. He was shaken but recuperated fast and said. "Five billion dollars who ever heard of such sums? Crystal you know I am well connected but I have no money you are God's gift to me in my old age. Write a check for ten million dollars and I will tell you the true story why Mr. Iho turned bad."

"Ancient-san I only have six million in this checking account. I will give you five million of it. Tell me why I should go home."

The old man became greedy he asked for six million or no story. Suki became nervous she started fidgeting with her purse again. The sake must have gotten to her, because she had trouble opening the zipper. I took the purse away from her and found Brown's gun in it. I don't know how she got it through customs. I took the gun out and put it in my lap. I was sitting in the lotus position. The old man was sitting on his heels comfortably."

"I can't because if I write a check for more than five million on this account alarms go off in Barclay's Bank and security checks in."

"Perhaps after you hear my story you will write a check for six million and let your security handle the situation." He saw Crystal's defiant look and said. "Never mind, I will take the five million and let you go your way. You are avenging angels I could tell the minute I saw the changes in Suki."

"Lila is mad at your father Suki he has a new Geisha who takes up more and more of your father's time. But first things first Crystal make out the check for five million dollars I will fill in the 'to' part of the check in Japanese if that is OK."

"It cannot be done. I have to fill out the whole thing in my hand my estate manager won't approve it otherwise. It will probably take a week to get the money transferred to your account."

The old man whispered his name and title in Crystal's ear. Crystal's eyes widened, "you are that close to the Emperor?"

He glanced at Suki but she was snoring softly sitting on her heels. "No wonder doors open for you. How come you don't have money?"

The old man sighed, "We were heavily invested in Korea and lost everything when Japan lost the colony. My father was stupid he put all his eggs in one basket."

Our Guru Prakash Piri appeared out of thin air. It was like watching him on television. He didn't talk in our minds we all heard his words.

Piri told Suki to look at the check. Suki looked at the check and asked Crystal. "Why are you giving the old man ten million dollars? Here Joseph look at it it's made out for ten million dollars."

I looked at the check and sure enough it was made out for ten million dollars. I handed it to Crystal who said. "I don't know what you guys are talking about I see five million dollars."

Suki grabbed the check and ripped it to shreds. Piri told Crystal to go in to the last bedroom pretty far away from where we were sitting and write the check there.

Crystal came back with the check. Suki and I looked at the check it was made out for five million dollars.

The Ancient said, "a lie for a lie," When you told me that you could not write a check for more than five million dollars I had an intuition that you were lying. I am an old man I can tell when someone is lying from sheer experience there is no magic to that at all."

Crystal handed him the five million dollar check. "I don't know how you did it but it better not happen again you can't seem to control all four of us that includes Piri, one of us will beat you up. Ancient laughed but his eyes did not. He started his story.

"As I told you Suki your mother is worried about your father's new Geisha, your father has stopped coming home, for weeks at a time.

"I checked with a contact in the police department who dealt with Geishas and whores in general.

"Miss Susie Park is a Japanese Korean not Geisha at all. She is a regular streetwalker who made good. She is under the protection of a gangster named Charles Iho.

"I went back to my contact to find out who Charles Iho was, his family background and such."

"My contact hit a brick wall. He had common information about his gangster activates but nothing of his background or family. Charles' specializes in whores male and female and owns three old Geishas schools.

He appeared six years ago as a full blown gangster according to the police computer. That was around the time Miss Susie Park showed up on the police computer too."

"She and Charles were arrested for robbing a tourist from Yokohama. I spoke to the arresting officer. He told me the case stuck in his mind, because Pimps never got involved in such blatant shakedowns. He got the impression that Charles and Susie wanted to get arrested they wanted to make a name for themselves in the underworld fast."

"It must have worked because Charles is considered the top pimp in Tokyo. He runs his business out of company a called Iho Forklift owned by his Uncle Sikura Iho."

"Iho Forklift Company and Mr. Sikura Iho are a very respectable in Japanese business circles. You know children life is odd, because I have known Sikura Iho for fifty years and never knew that he had nephew. He is a founding member of our society. I collected oddities when I was younger, he was a famous gambler and womanizer, just right for my club. He would travel to Europe and America to gamble and come back with big busted European girls."

"In Lila's behalf I called on him. I have not seen him in five years. He is not aging well all those nights gambling are taking their toll. He is a bit senile not that you notice if you did not know him."

"When I brought up Charles he was quite happy to talk about him. He said Charles was his cousin's son who showed up on his doorstep thirty years ago broke, and without a home, his mother a high class Geisha in a small town died of consumption."

"Charles was ten years old. He had a letter from his mother begging Iho to take care of him. He bundled the kid off to military school and forgot about him."

"Three years ago Charles showed up again with a badly bruised face a broken arm and a broken leg. He had a strange story. He said he worked for the Japanese equivalent of the CIA. He was trained in all the marshal arts and spy craft necessary for a "hood" a muscle boy. Charles was quite proud that he was not a deskman but an agent on the front lines."

"Charles was quite honest with old man Sikura. He said he was recruited when he was in his last year of high school. He was trained for two years and sent to a South Korean University to learn Korean. He fell in with a bad crowd gangsters and whores."

"His case officer decided that his talents were with the muscle boys not with political analysis they brought him back and taught him every dirty trick a field agent needs."

"He lived in South Korea for fifteen years under an assumed name developing friendship with South Korean black marketers who did business with North Korea."

"Everything worked fine until he developed a crack cocaine habit. He met a Korean whore who was into crack. She was a cheap whore servicing American soldiers who came to Seoul on leave. The American soldiers sold her crack. Charles liked the habit. It made him feel like a superman he and Susie Park became an item in the South Korean underworld."

"His case officer noticed the change Charles was becoming violent. His case officers started hearing rumors of a Japanese man and a Korean woman ripping off whorehouses with extreme violence."

"His case officer put two and two together and sent him to the United States for a month the rip-offs stopped in Seoul. His case officer confronted him and ordered him to return to Japan. Charles refused to go without Susie Park. His case officer agreed if they both went into rehabilitation for their crack addiction. Charles went trough rehab with flying colors. Susie Park switched to powdered cocaine, which made her less violent and took her off the radar screen of the spy agency."

The Ancient continued. "For some reason, that I don't understand The Japanese spy agency sends large sums of money to North Korea through Japanese Koreans. The agency's paymaster among the Japanese Koreans was a gangster who died suddenly. They filled the void with Charles who was back to his old 'good loyal' self."

"He must be stupid, because he was back with Susie Park and the cocaine habit. Cocaine is very expansive in Japan. Charles was making money as a gangster but it wasn't enough. Charles put Susie Park on the payroll as courier. His new handler in Japan didn't realize how dangerous this was when he approved her employment."

"She and Charles started stealing some of the money that was supposed to go to North Korea. It took the North Koreans three years before they figured out the scam. The North Koreans are a hard lot. They sent a squad of specialist to Tokyo and gave Charles and Susie Park the beating of their lives.

"Why didn't they kill them?" Suki asked. I could tell she was getting bored with the story.

"They didn't kill them, because the gangster setup is very good Charles and Susie Park learned their lesson, they stayed away from cocaine and delivered the money religiously. But I am getting ahead of myself."

"Badly beaten Charles showed up on old man Iho's doorstep. Old men like to be needed so he hired Charles as an accountant for Iho Forklift Company.

"It didn't take long for Charles to figure out that Iho Forklift Company did not make enough money for the old man's four million a year gambling habit.

"He pressured the old man for the real story. After keeping the story secret for almost sixty years Sikura Iho was happy to tell the story to a relative. He figured Charles would take over his position after he died anyway.

"Crystal do you have a man named Peter Henderson working for you?"

"Yes, he keeps Mr. Iho happy. He delivers Iho's money every quarter."

Suki had enough, she shouted. "What about my father? How the hell does he fit into this story?"

"According to Mr. Iho your father and Mr. Sikura Iho belong to the same businessmen's club. Your family's company rents Iho forklifts. Mr. Iho introduced Charles to your father and in turn Charles introduced Susie Park to your father. She and your father hit if off, he pays for her apartment and living expenses."

"That is all. No blackmail or anything?" Suki asked suspiciously.

"Not far as Mr. Iho knows."

"Let me talk about Mr. Henderson Suki. He is your Trojan horse Crystal."

"Don't tell me an employee who is with my firm for twenty five years sold me out?"

"He didn't have much of a choice. Charles likes to brag so he told his uncle everything. Mr. Iho, who is an honest man, is full of guilt. That is why he told me everything."

"Mr., Henderson killed Susie Park. It is the oldest trick in the spy business. Man goes out with a woman he gets very drunk. He remembers that he and the woman got into an argument but that is all he remembers. He is woken up by the screaming of a maid."

Crystal interrupted, "I know the scam Henderson finds her dead body and Charles comes into the room calms the maid down and proposes to take care of the matter for a price. What did he do with the body?"

The Ancient laughed. "There was no body. Susie Park was injected with a drug that made her stiff and cool. She came out of it in a couple of hours. Evidently she dies regularly for Charles."

"Who else did they compromise in my company? Henderson is a well-paid messenger boy. He knows nothing of the business." Crystal demanded.

"Do you know a Mr. John Wells?" the old man asked.

Crystal bit her lower lip and said. "Yes he is the Vice President of the Asia desk. I assume Susie Park died for him too. What a scam Brown would have loved it. Wells probably gave Charles Iho a complete picture of my Japanese operation. I wonder how Wells got a hold of my Iho Forklift stocks?"

"William and I are the only ones who have the combination to the safe holding the stocks. Charles is probably like Chin an expert safe cracker. When did this operation take place?"

"According to Sikura Iho two and a half years ago." The Ancient answered obviously enjoying his role.

"William and I checked the stocks last year. I have a million shares. I didn't count them of course. Each certificate is worth a thousand shares. Charles is a smart guy, who would notice ten certificates are missing. They are old fashioned bearer stocks my name is not on them. Who has them owns them. Williams had a code printed on each one in invisible ink thank God for William and his suspicious mind. How much did Toyota pay for the ten thousand shares?"

The old man laughed. "Charles Iho did not sell him the stocks. He gave the stocks to Toyota as collateral for a fifty million dollar loan. Wells' gave a printout of all your holdings to Charles. Mr. Toyota read the report and made the loan to Iho Forklift."

"Charles Iho bought two defunct hospitals in the United States and refurbished them then leased them to a consortium of doctors on the condition that Toyota's pharmaceutical company supplied all the disposable products and medication. Iho Forklift Company gets a cut of that too."

Crystal looked at me and asked. "What do you think of this Joseph?"

I replied. "Do you have the rest of the stocks?"

"Yes."

I continued. "Then you own a lot of hospitals in the United States, because he made the deals through Iho Forklift Company. Charles Iho is a very bright guy. Your best bet is to hire him. Put him in the golden cage of money. Does John Wells know who you are?"

"We never met. All my orders go through paperwork, William might know him."

Suki started laughing and said. "The man with the biggest penis in the world called cocaine the golden cage. Funny you should use term Joseph."

"I told Suki testily that I meant money greenbacks yens not drugs." Suki just laughed.

The Ancient got up and said. "It's not a bad idea to hire Charles Iho. By the way how did you find out Iho Forklift Company was infiltrated?"

Crystal replied laughing. "We went to Miami on a plane owned by Toyota Pharmaceuticals; it got into an accident. My dear friend Suki mentioned that the plane was leased from Iho Forklift Company. It was a shock to me, because I own Iho Forklift and had no reports that it was in the business of leasing planes. I do own planes but that is under Iho Leasing Service, which Mr. Sikura Iho knew nothing about. So here we are. I don't want to cause Suki's father trouble so we are handling this business ourselves."

The Ancient said. "I will arrange for you to meet Charles and Sikura tomorrow at a very nice restaurant where you can talk. By the way Charles's Japanese first name is Akira, 'bright boy' I think he deserves the name. Meanwhile Elvis is waiting for me. Do you want to come along Suki? He is quite nice you know we can have a threesome."

"With that little creep never."

The old man kissed the check Crystal gave him and left with new strength in his step.

I could not sleep nor did the girls. We got stinking drunk and the three of us had sex for the first time; we had fun.

The Ancient called and told us to meet him at a restaurant named Tokyo Express he arranged for a private room.

I put my three million in a safe located in the bathroom; Suki had the safe's code from her mother Lila, which she gave to me, but not to Crystal. I wanted to put the cocaine in the garbage but Suki would not hear of it. "It is mine." She said. "I earned it the hard way, a very hard way." Who could argue with that?

Suki got a cloth shopping bag and brought the cocaine with us to the restaurant. She said pointedly. "I don't want anybody throwing it in the garbage when I am not looking."

Suki spoke to the hostess who led us to a private room. We sat on the floor around a table. In the center of the table there was a grill low gas flames were shooting out of it. Plates full of chicken breast, Kobi beef and assorted vegetables were around the grill.

The Ancient showed us how to eat while we were waiting for Charles and Mr. Sikura Iho to show up.

The door opened and an old man with a cane entered followed by a roly-poly man. I expected a Japanese James Bond but this guy looked like somebody's favorite uncle. He carried a laptop computer. He apologized profusely for being late but Mr. Sikura Iho did not feel well.

Charles ordered each of us a quart bottle of sake. The Ancient ordered us in mind speak not to drink anything. I looked at Charles and Mr. Iho. "Don't worry Joseph they can't hear. I know it is hard to believe but very few people in Japan can. Stop fidgeting with that bag Suki."

Suki said in mind speak "Up yours Ancient." But she stopped messing with the bag.

After we ate our full of the food we cooked on the grill, Charles offered us drinks, but we declined to drink. However, Charles and the two old men drank like fish. Charles asked. "Is everybody full?" We all agreed we had enough to eat. He opened the laptop and said. "Then we can get down to business," in good business English.

Crystal looked at the laptop asked. "What am I looking at?"

"You are looking at Iho Forklift Companies' new holdings, fifty hospitals in the USA, twenty five Medivac helicopters, and ten Medivac planes. We have enough cash on hand to pay Toyota Pharmaceuticals back the fifty million seed money and we still have six hundred million dollars' worth of property and cash in the bank. The Ancient told me how you found out about me. Well bad luck for me good luck for you."

"I am ready to make a deal. You hire me at the same rate you pay my uncle and indemnify me against prosecution then you can have all of it without a fight and I will work for you loyally as my uncle does."

Crystal said. "Ok, you are hired but your pay will be decided by my Compensation Committee. I have no idea what you are worth."

Old man Iho hugged Charles and said, "I thank thousand Buddha's for everything working out alright."

Suki screeched. "It worked out eh? What about my father and Susie Park Mr. Charles?"

Charles said. "You know Japanese culture Suki. Your father and Susie Park have an arrangement. I don't know what she likes in a sixty-four year old man but she dropped me for him."

The Ancient said in mind speak. "He is lying but don't push it something is up. I am going to the bathroom."

After the Ancient left Suki said "There must be something you can do Charles you are her pimp. Charles got beet purple in the face and shouted. "I am her lover not her pimp and I am telling you she left me for your father."

"I got something for you Charles Akira Iho." Suki whispered.

She pulled out the kilo of cocaine. "A kilo of cocaine, you can have it just get Susie Park out of my father's life."

"No." old man Iho shouted and tried to push the package of cocaine into the grill. Charles pushed the old man back roughly.

"A kilo of cocaine just for that? Maybe something can be done after all, let me taste it, Suki."

He stuck a plastic chopstick in the package. White powder came out of the hole. Charles formed a line cocaine and sniffed it up with a rolled up yen note.

"Very-very-very good stuff, that's for a fact, Suki. You know Eric Clapton's song Cocaine? You know where he sings that cocaine never lies. Well I don't know why I need you assholes anyway?"

He hit his right arm with his left hand and a gun came out of his right sleeve into his right hand. The first shot hit me in the chest the second shot hit Crystal in the chest and the third shot got Suki in the chest. Old man Iho wailed, "Akira no!"

I found myself sitting in the cross-legged position in the Thousand Petal Lotus. Suki was on the left of me and Crystal was on my right, Prakash Piri was in front of us.

Guru Piri said, "you couldn't keep your mouth shut could you Suki? You had to give cocaine to an animal! You guys can't die just yet. I want you three to be there when I open our ashram in Rajastan. I found a beautiful place on a lake."

I said laughing. "How do we survive getting shot in the heart? The bastard is a damn good shot."

Guru Piri laughed and said. "There is town called Pushkar in India. It has the one and only temple dedicated to Brahma the creative force of the universe. Inside Brahma's Temple there is a turtle inscribed on the floor. You will find yourselves standing on its shell."

"A Brahmin priest will come up to you tell him what happened and if he likes your story he will send you back with a solution to your problem, otherwise, he will send you on to your next reincarnation which would be too bad, because I would like to have you three in this world."

We found ourselves standing on the turtle stark naked. An old man came up to us and said. "Shame on you Suki you must learn to control your temper or you will be back here no time at all and you three will be reborn as a crows. It will be many rebirths before you become human again. He threw a powder on us and we found ourselves sitting looking at Charles Iho. He was bug eyed.

"I just shot you three to death. I never miss. Where the hell is the cocaine?"

"What cocaine?" Suki asked innocently. "There is no cocaine you just drank too much Charles. You are imagining things Charlie-san." She rubbed his stomach, which I didn't like too much.

He picked up the gun from the table. "I shot you guys. I saw you die."

He ejected the magazine they were loaded with blanks. "Shit I must have picked up the wrong magazine. Sometimes Susie Park and I use blanks in our con-games."

Suddenly Charles started looking around wildly. "Where is the computer? It was right here."

We heard the Ancient's voice in mind-speak. "I don't know how it happened but the computer ended up with me when I left the room. Tell him I have it. He won't dare to mess with me. You will have to write another check for five million if you want the laptop Crystal."

Crystal laughed out loud and said in mind-speak. "So you made up your mind to get ten million from me you Ancient derelict?"

The Ancient answered in mind-speak, "Yes, Joseph tell Charles-san that I am sitting in his Boss's house. He will understand that I am talking to his case officer."

Charles was full of piss and vinegar until my cell phone rang. I closed the phone and told him it was the Ancient sitting in his boss's house. The change on Charlie-san was dramatic. He shrunk in his suit.

Suki piped up. "Can you find it in your heart to call Susie Park away from my father forever Charlie-san. In fact we would like to see her go back to South Korea, you can make that happen can't you Charlie-san?"

The Ancient said in mind-speak, "Joseph tell him the Boss says if he is still Crystal's employee then he should prove his loyalty to Crystal by going to Susie Park's apartment and giving Susie Park the bad news that she has to go back to South Korea."

I said in mind-speak. "I can't do it Ancient-san. I have a feeling he is going to kill us before he betrays Susie Park."

"Don't worry Joseph Susie Park is dead for real. Just send Charlie Iho out of the restaurant thinking everything is alright. There are ten of his case officer's 'hoods' waiting for him outside; he is already dead just waiting for the bullet to hit him. If I had stayed he would have shot me, a big mistake on his part, I intend to live a few more years to enjoy my new found riches."

"Leave the check on Lila's old dressing table Crystal. You three go to New York on the next plane and the laptop will follow you. Tell Guru Piri his got my respect; Sayonara."

My cell phone rang. I turned to Charlie Iho and said, "It's the Ancient. He says your boss will forgive everything if Crystal employs you." Charlie gave Crystal a pleading look.

Crystal said. "Sure, you are my employee Charlie-san, you made a lot of money for me. Go ahead Joseph tell them he is my employee shooting us was just a big joke wasn't it Charlie-san?"

Charlie Iho picked up his uncle who passed out.

Suki asked. "Why don't you leave old man Iho with us? Let him sleep it off here. You just go over to Susie Park's house and take care of business."

Charlie mumbled, "Sure, I'll leave him here and go to Susie Park's house she will understand."

I said. "Sayonara Charlie-san." Charlie left us on numb wooden legs.

The sound of gunshots reached our ears. A young woman dressed in a flashy evening gown opened the door to our cubicle. "Would you believe it? A famous gangster just got killed outside of the restaurant. Perhaps you three should leave before the newspapers show up. I will take care of Mr. Iho."

Suki asked belligerently. "Who are you?"

The young Japanese woman replied in good English laughing. "Who are you? Isn't that what the Caterpillar asked Alice when she was ten inches tall?

"I killed Susie Park, it was a long time coming, I enjoyed it. I shot her in the head through her apartment window with a scope rifle while she was riding your father. Your father was too drunk to know the difference. My boss's boys removed her body; in a week your father will wonder whatever happened to his favorite girl."

Suki gave the young woman the finger which turned into a hug then we left the restaurant for Crystal's place through the backdoor.

Riding in the taxi I called Japan Airlines and reserved first class tickets for three on the businessmen's red-eye flight to New York. But before I confirmed it Suki said. "My father has a flight going to New York at midnight." I cancelled the Japan Airline's flight and asked Suki. "What happened to the cocaine?"

She answered laughing. "Didn't you notice Joseph, old Mr. Iho used it as a pillow. The woman who killed Susie Park probably has it now. She will probably steal it. But it's Ok; I have ninety-nine more packages in Florida."

Crystal and Suki bickered over who owned what in Florida. I closed my eyes and the tension drained from my body. I let my mind wonder about Guru Piri, the Thousand Petal Lotus and the Brahmin Temple in Pushkar, India. Life is strange it flows like a never ending river on and on forever.

Author. Rabbi Thomas Muhlrad
2000 to April 11, 2009